Gabriel
A Story Of The Jews In Prague

By

S. Kohn

Double9 BOOKS

Gabriel
A Story Of The Jews In Prague
by S. Kohn

ISBN: 978-93-61153-29-7

Published by

DOUBLE 9 BOOKS
2/13-B, Ansari Road
Daryaganj, New Delhi – 110002
info@double9books.com
www.double9books.com
Tel. 011-40042856

ABOUT THE AUTHOR

The world has been captivated by the creative talents of renowned novelist S. Kohn. S. Kohn's writing skilfully blends wit, inventiveness, and eloquence to produce intricate tales that transport readers to incredible locations. Their writing style is distinguished by its poetic prose, vivid descriptions, and in-depth analysis of the human condition. Whether delving deeply into historical events or conjuring up fantastical worlds, S. Kohn has a remarkable ability to write engrossing stories that fascinate readers. Through his thought-provoking subjects and well-developed characters, S. Kohn leads readers on a tour of self-discovery while challenging social norms and presenting fresh perspectives. S. Kohn was a master communicator and storyteller who woven words into a narrative that appeals to people of all ages and backgrounds. Writing is a personal dance between creativity and discipline, and it carries the weight of not only telling tales but also influencing viewpoints and igniting discussions.

CONTENTS

Chapter I

It was the morning of a wintry autumnal day in the year 1620, when a young man stepped slowly and thoughtfully through the so-called Pinchas-Synagogue Gate into the Jews' quarter in the city of Prague. A strange scene presented itself. The morning service was just over in the synagogues, and whilst numerous crowds were still streaming out of the houses of prayer, others, mostly women with heavy bunches of keys in their hands, were already hurrying to the rag-market situated outside of the Ghetto. The shops too and stalls within the Ghetto were now opened, and even in the open street an activity never seen in the other quarters of the city displayed itself. Here, for instance, dealers--in truth of the lowest class--were offering their wares consisting of pastry, wheat-bread, fruits, cheese, cabbage, boiled peas and more of such kind of stuff to the passers-by. Here and there too in spite of the early hour emerged some peripatetic cooks, in peaceful competition extolling loudly the products of their kitchen, bits of liver, eggs, meat and puddings, and whilst in one hand they held a tin plate, in the other a two-pronged fork,--a very unnecessary article for most of their guests,--devoted their attention chiefly to the foreign students of the Talmud. To them also the greatest attention was paid by those cobblers who less wealthy than their colleagues in the so-called Golden St. offered their services to the students in open street, and most assiduously, while the owners were obliged to wait in the street or a neighbouring house, mended their shoes at a very moderate price, but, it must also be allowed, in a very inefficient manner.

The young man who had just stepped into the Jew's quarter, gazed earnestly and observantly at this busy stir, and did not seem to notice, that he himself had become an object of common attention. His appearance was however fully calculated to excite observation. His form was powerful and commanding; his dress that of a Talmud-student, cloak and cap. Out of his pale face shadowed by a dark beard, under heavy arching eyebrows there shone two black eyes of uncommon brilliance; raven locks fell in waves from his head; the fingers of a white sinewy hand, that held close the silken cloak, were covered with golden rings; his thick ruff was of spotless purity and smoothness. Had not the stranger by the elegance of his appearance, perhaps also by his gigantic make, struck a little awe into the curious dealers in the street, of a surety at his first appearance, a whole heap of questions would have been addressed to him. "Who or what he wanted? What could they do for him?" and such like.... Under the circumstances, however, it was Abraham, a cobbler, who sat on a bench by the Pinchas-Synagogue that after some consideration mustered up courage and as he laid down a shoe that had been committed to his artistic skill, began to ask: "dear student! whom are you seeking? Certainly not me, that I can see from your beautifully made shoes with their glittering silver buckles; *they* were not made at Prague."--This was put in more for the benefit of those about him and himself than the stranger.--"You are surely a stranger here? pardon me, you are perhaps a German, a Moravian or a Viennese? do you wish to go to a lecture upon the Talmud, or perchance to the Rabbi, or to Reb Lippman Heller? Who do you want to go to? I will gladly shew you the way to the Talmud-lecturers--or, perhaps, you are looking out for a lodging? I can very likely procure you a convenient one." "I *am* a stranger here," replied the student, "and must, indeed, first of all look about me for a lodging. If you happen to know of an apartment where I could pursue my studies undisturbed I shall thankfully avail myself of your offer: but the apartment must be large, light and cheerful."

"Then I only know of one in the whole town, at my superior attendant Reb Schlome's, I mean the superior attendant of my synagogue, the Old-Synagogue, he lives close to the synagogue; there is a beautiful room there--and besides, Reb Schlome is very learned in the Talmud, and has got a beautiful library,--in a word that or none is the lodging for you."

While this short conversation was going on, the cobbler's neighbours had as it were accidentally got nearer, so as to overhear a few words; and the group that for some minutes had been hazarding the most ingenious opinions and conjectures about the stranger, formed, perhaps without noticing it, a complete circle round the two talkers. This was now suddenly broken through, and a shabbily dressed old man thrust himself up impetuously against the stranger.

"Peace be with you," he cried, "you are then just arrived, be so good as to come with me, I have a question to put to you, it will do you no harm, and me good, come with me."

The stranger gazed in astonishment at the singular figure. "What do you want of me? How can I, a stranger, whom you have surely never seen, give you any tidings? perhaps, however, you do know me?"

"Sir," whispered Cobbler Abraham, standing on tiptoe so as to reach up to the stranger's ear, "Jacob is out of his mind; ten years ago, when he came to live at Prague, he used to put the strangest questions to everybody that came in his way; when the small boys came out of the school, he used to examine them in the Bible, and however correctly they answered, would ever become furious and cry: False! False!--grown-up people too he used to catechise, fathers, students, in short every one; but as he has now put his questions to almost everybody in the whole community, he has kept quite quiet for a long while. He is only unsociable, refuses to give any information about himself, and never answers a question; but he is a good harmless fellow, and as the students say, must be a very great Talmudist--I wonder that he begins again."--

"Don't be led astray by what that man there is whispering to you," cried the old man in anguish; "only come with me, I pray you most instantly to do so--you, only you can give me peace; I will believe your answers, all the rest lie to me, a poor old man! Come home with me, believe me, you will do a real good deed."

The stranger cast a penetrating searching glance at the old man, as though he would sound the whole depths of this troubled human soul. Contrary to all expectation he replied after short reflection: "only unloose my cloak; hold me not so nervously, I will verily go with you. But to you," he turned to the cobbler, "I will soon come back, and will then beg you to conduct me to the man who has the room to let. Accept this in the meanwhile for your friendly sympathy"--as he spoke he drew out of his doublet an embroidered purse full of gold and silver pieces, and laid a large silver coin on the cobbler's bench. "That is too much," said Abraham highly surprised and pleased, "God strengthen you, your Honour, Reb--I don't know what's your name!"--

Without answering these further questions, the stranger stepped by the side of the old man out of the circle, which now once more began loudly and without circumlocution to utter its conjectures.

"I know what he is:--he is a fool," suggested a dealer in liver as she arranged her stores on a board--"and what's more a big fool! gives Abraham a piece of silver, what for? goes home with the madman, why?"

"My dear Mindel," urged another huckster, "it seems to me you are very envious of Abraham; that's why the handsome stranger student is a fool. If you'd got the money, he would have been wise!"--

Most of the hucksters, and hucksteresses, seemed fully to concur in the opinion of the fish-monger--such was the speaker--for Mother Mindel was in truth what one would in these days in popular parlance call a dog in the manger. But Mother Mindel was not the sort of person in a war of words to leave the lists in a hurry, and own herself vanquished. She answered therefore sharply: "Say you so, Hirsch, what did you get from him. Come now, tell the truth." These last words spoken in a somewhat high key, can only be understood when it is explained, that Hirsch, the fish-monger, was too often addicted to the bad habit, when he told a story, of passing off in fullest measure the exaggerations and embellishments of his copious imagination; of treating, on the other hand, an actual fact in a very step-motherish fashion, a circumstance that compelled even his best friends to admit that he was a little given to exaggeration; while impartial persons were fond of applying to him the well-deserved predicate of 'liar.'

"If I'm to tell the truth," continued Hirsch, apparently not observing that which was injurious in his neighbour's manner of expressing herself, "If I'm to tell the truth I'm not so envious as some people, who seem to have been created so by the dear God, probably as a punishment; I should, however, have been more pleased if Pradel, the pastry-cook, had got the money, she has five children, her husband, the bass-singer in the Old-Synagogue, is away, lying ill at home for the last four months--*she* would have made a better use of the money--but if it had rained gold the good woman would not have been at the place, and if she had, what would have been the use? would *she* have had the impudence at once coolly to accost a stranger with gold rings on his fingers like a prince as if he was a nobody? Why did we all hold our tongues? I was only curious to see how far Cobbler Abrabam would go. A very little more and he'd have asked him the name of his great-grandfathers, how long it was since his thirteenth birthday, and what chapter out of the prophets had at that time been read on the Sabbath."--

These words seemed to show that the brave Hirsch in addition to his unpleasant habit of exaggeration could not be altogether absolved from the failing of his neighbour Mindel.--In the bosom of Cobbler Abraham who had listened to all these gibes in silence some significant idea seemed striving for utterance. He moved uneasily on his stool and rubbed his hands with a singular smile.

"Good people!" he cried at length, "I'll show you that none of you yet know Cobbler Abraham, although for now more than twenty years he has enjoyed the great honour in your society of mending shoes for the scholars at the high school of Prague, and for more than twenty years has had the privilege of listening to your lies, Hirsch, and to your tattle, Mindel. None of you yet know Cobbler Abraham. The money I shall consider as if it was not mine. It belongs to Pradel the pastry-cook, or rather to her sick husband Simche, he's my bass, that is, bass of my synagogue, has never in his life got a new year's or other present from me. I'm a bachelor, he's a married man with five children: I'm, thank God, in good health, he's ill. I for once will be a prince, he shall have the money from me, at once, to-day, as a dedicatory gift, and as to your insinuation Hirsch, that none of you had the impudence to accost the stranger, perhaps, you would be more justified in saying that none of you had had the sense to do it; and now, seeing that I'll have none of the money, leave me alone, let me get on with my work, and sell your sweet fish and roast liver." So saying he caught briskly up the shoes that were before him, and began industriously to cobble.

"Ah, there's some sense in that, I knew you had a good heart;" even Mother Mindel was obliged to join in the loud applause of the neighbours, whereupon she tried to secure an honourable retreat out of the wordy skirmish by kindling with the whole strength of her lungs into a bright glow the fading flame of her charcoal pan; whilst, Hirsch, after he too had in an embarrassed way recognised Abraham's noble feeling, availed himself of that very moment as the most favourable to recommend his fish to the passers-by, as especially excellent.--But the three neighbours were of a very placable disposition, and in spite of the fact that they had for the last ten years followed the laudable custom, of jeering as opportunity offered, yet in time of need and wretchedness they had mutually stood by one another, and so it came to pass, that half an hour after, they had forgotten the little dispute, but not its cause; and the three neighbours were laying their heads together to ventilate anew their, doubtless very interesting surmises about the stranger.

He meanwhile was walking in silence by the side of his strange companion, and though he looked about inquisitively, still found time to observe Jacob more closely. It was difficult to fix the old man's age. His pale countenance was sorrow-stricken, and furrowed by care. It might once have been beautiful but was transformed into something different, strange, scarce akin to a human face by a grizzly white untended beard, that entangled with the disordered hair, which fell in waves from his head, formed with it a shapeless mass; but especially by the weird glittering of his eyes that protruded far out of their sockets. His thin form crushed by the weight of misery, seemed once to have been gigantic, and the scantiness of his clothing completed the singular impression caused by his appearance. At the Hahn-alley the old man stopped before a small house, and begged the stranger to follow him across the court to his little room. It was poorly furnished, and situated on the ground floor, abutting the burial-ground, so that one could without difficulty pass through the low window into the burial-ground. Besides an arm-chair there was only one stool in the room. The old man pushed both up silently to the table, and signed to the stranger to take a seat.

"What do you wish?" the stranger now asked. The old man looked cautiously about to see if anyone was listening, closed the door, then the window-shutters and lit a lamp. "See," he now began, "see, as I looked at you, it affected me so differently, impressed me so far otherwise than when

I look at any other strange student. I know you are not so wicked as the others are, all, all of them, that despise, ill use, unsparingly laugh to scorn a poor old man; they know no pity, have no mercy, are not aware what it is to suffer as I suffer. They bring me to naught, they have all sworn together against me, and whom ever I question, he answers falsely, falsely, falsely!"--

The old man spoke with frightful excitement, all the blood that flowed through his withered body seemed to have gathered itself into his cheeks flushed with a hectic red, the veins of his forehead swelled to an unnatural size. "Tell me, tell me, tell me truly," he whispered, suddenly becoming again quite humble. "Do you know the ten commandments? but I conjure you by the God of Israel, that made heaven and earth, by the head of your father, by your mother's salvation, by your portion in the world to come, answer truly, without deceit."

"My good old man," said the stranger quietly, "I will do all that you desire, I will repeat to you the ten commandments, all the six hundred and thirteen laws, provided always, I can still recollect them, I will be entirely at your service, for I see, that you are a poor worn-out man--you live pretty well alone here in this narrow room, you receive no visits?" asked the student after a short pause.

"Since I have found out that no one will come home with me, to read me the ten commandments out of my small Bible, I let no one in. Many too are afraid--no one comes to me, no one, you are the first that for many years has set foot in my hovel.--But now be so good, let me hear the ten commandments, quickly, I implore you!"

The young man passed his hand over his forehead, as though he would call back to memory something long forgotten, and then began in a loud powerful voice to utter by heart those ten sayings of the Lord, that were revealed on Sinai. The old man sat resting his head which he bent forward upon both hands--as though greedily to suck up every word that fell from his lips--and gazed into the face of the stranger. All the blood seemed to flow back slowly to his heart, his face became deadly pale, his eyes seemed bursting from their wide opened lids, and the longer the stranger spoke, the deeper blue became his thin spasmodically quivering lips. Had not the beating of the tortured old man's heart been audible, one must have believed that life was extinct in that frail body. The stranger went quietly on, but as he uttered the seventh commandment '*Thou shalt not commit adultery*' a fearfully horrible cry, a cry that made the very bones creep, escaped from the breast of the poor tormented creature, a cry shrill as that which, a bird of prey sore wounded by an arrow, launches through the air in its death struggles, a cry, such as naught but the deepest most unspeakable grief of the soul can tear from a man's breast. The stranger stopped, the old man sank in a heap, covering his face with both hands. There was a moment of deepest silence, at length the old man broke forth into loud sobbing.--

"You too! I had hope of you. Oh, how I would have loved you, how I would have honoured you, how I would have worshipped you, if you had read differently to the others, but no, no, no! *he* read. Thou shalt not commit adultery. "*Thou shalt not commit adultery.*' Lord of the World, have I suffered too little, repented too little, done insufficient penitence? And yet Thou still lettest it stand in Thy holy scripture? Must I for ever be tormented in this world and the next? But Thou art righteous, and I a sinner--I have sinned, I have gone astray, I have"--then beating his breast he muttered the whole confession of sins.

"I grieve to have been the cause of pain to you, but see"--the student at these words opened a Bible that was lying on the table at the passage in point--"see, it is as I have read it." The characters were quite effaced by the marks of tears, and it was clear that this especial page had been read and reread countless times.

"Yes, yes, so is it written," cried the old man in a tone of the profoundest dejection and despair. "You were right, *my brother* was right, all were right, the students, the little boys from school, all, all read it so--all are right, except me, except me,--I am guilty!"--and again he began, striking both his clenched hands upon his breast, to utter the confession.

The student had risen from his seat, and paced the chamber up and down. The old man's illimitable grief seemed to awaken a slight feeling of sympathy in him. "Every one is not like thee, a giant in spirit and thought," said he softly to himself, "every one cannot like thee strip off his faith like a raiment that has become useless, and rouse a new life from the inner fire of the soul." The man was not always mad, a milder light must once have shone out of those weird dark eyes--*but he sank through his own guilt!* One bold flight of his free spirit had saved him from everlasting night, but he would not! Was he constrained to give credence to a dead word out of the Bible? Did he stand upon flaming Sinai, when the words were thundered down upon humanity? Could not he free himself from the blind faith of his fathers? Must that appear to him true and holy, that appeared true and holy to his father and forefathers? His fathers ecstatically smiling could mount the smoking pyres, and while flames consumed their body, sing psalms and hymns of praise, *they* could do all this for they looked for the bliss of Paradise in a world they hoped to come: and what is the bitterest, saddest moment of torment compared with an eternity that never ends! His fathers could breath out their lives with a smile under the axe of the persecutor; with faith they had life's highest gift, Hope. But this fool? He has sinned, good!--tear then from thy lacerated and bleeding heart the foolish faith, that torments thee, what good does it do thee, thou poor lost one, in this world or the next?--Yet there is a mighty too constraining power in Faith!----"How if *I* tried yet to believe?--the sweet fable can heal wounds too!--but I, I cannot, I cannot--they have cast me forth, they have compelled me to it, the Bible, men--all, all--I, indeed, *I* could not otherwise."

Then he stopped again suddenly before the old man, who without paying further attention to his guest, had lapsed into a gloomy brooding.

"Of course, you are a Talmudist?" asked the student aloud, "you are! Now then, know you not the sentence of the pious king Chiskia? Though a sharp sword lyeth at the neck of man, yet may he not despair of God's infinite mercy! Do not forget: in the same chapter in which it is written 'Thou shalt not commit adultery' it is also written: 'The Lord, the Lord God, merciful and gracious, long suffering and abundant in goodness and truth, keeping mercy for thousands, forgiving iniquity and transgression and sin!'"--

"But he visits the iniquity of the fathers upon the children and upon the children's children unto the third and to the fourth generation!" said Jacob in continuation. "Do not despair! If the gates of prayer have been closed since the destruction of the sanctuary in Jerusalem, the gates of repentance have not been closed. Do not despair, poor Jacob, consider what the Bible says: 'For man's heart is wicked even from his youth up.' Consider the saying: 'As I live, saith the Lord God, I have no pleasure in the death of the wicked, but that the wicked turn from his way and live'; consider that well and do not despair!"--

The student broke off suddenly, as if astonished at the compassion that had been stirred up in him, it seemed to have surprised himself. But Jacob in the excess of his emotion clapsed the strangers' hand convulsively and pressed it to his lips.

"Ah, what good you do me," he cried; "how you drop balm into my irremediable wounds! For years no one has spoken to me thus; God bless you for it!" "You see, Jacob," said the student preparing to depart, "I have obeyed your request and have done you such service as I could.--It is now my turn to ask a favour of you.--No one comes to see you, you are often alone, suffer me occasionally to visit you and study the Talmud here. Perhaps I may be able to banish the evil spirit that at times seizes you."

"Oh, a wicked, wicked spirit, you are right.--Yes, you with your beautiful eyes you do me good.--Ah, once I too was as you are, tall, handsome, strong. When I gaze on you, I call to remembrance my own happy youth, my brother's! Yes, come to me often, often."

"That I will, and now farewell."

"God bless you."

The student stepped out of the house; then stood lost in thought. "I shall consider the chance a fortunate one," he softly said, "that led to my encounter with this madman; he may be useful to me, may put me upon the right track in my sublime chace. But it is inexplicable to me! I thought that I had quenched all compassion, all pity in my soul, and lo! this old man wakens feelings in me, that I would have banished for ever from my soul. Every one rejects him, and I, I who bear so bitter, so deadly a hatred against all those that hang on Bible texts, I let him immediately, before I saw my advantage therefrom, gain his end and placed myself at his disposal. Alas, in spite of the maddest hatred, the most raging fury, there is still too much of the good old Jew left in me. I must become very different."

Chapter II

Reb Schlome Sachs, superior attendant in the old synagogue, had on Friday evening just returned home from this synagogue. In his house and in his heart there ruled a Sabbath-peace. There is something very pleasurable in a small room on such a winter Friday evening! A large black stove radiated a pleasant warmth, whilst in the middle of the room a pendant lamp of eight branches, spread abroad a subdued, ruddy, but yet friendly light. On the oblong table lay a clean white cloth, under it again might be seen yet another particoloured covering, from the corners of which tassels were hanging and served as a cheerful pastime for a lively cat. But the loveliest ornament of the room was without a doubt the housewife Schöndel, a blooming graceful woman of about thirty. As she, in her elegant Sabbath-attire, the rich clusters of her dark hair becomingly covered by a richly worked cap, in her pretty, close fitting neatly made gown, fastened high up on the neck, stepped to meet her husband, and took off his cloak and cap, as they both of them joyously wished one another a happy Sabbath, as in their features a pure and childlike joyfulness of soul, a deep and blessed peace of mind mirrored itself--then surely would neither of them have exchanged their lot for that of kings or princes.

The master sang the Psalm of the day, and as he ended, enquired, "was Reb Gabriel not yet come home."

"No, he wished to go to-day to the old New-synagogue which he has not yet seen."

"Oh, then he will return later; we in the old synagogue only repeat the Friday-Psalm once and have no 'benediction.'--How do you like our new tenant that Cobbler Abraham brought us?"

"Oh, I like him very well, a handsome man of refined habits and demeanour; not at all like a Talmud-student; they think of nothing but their themes and disputations; but Reb Gabriel converses well and gracefully. He must be of a good and wealthy family; his deportment too is very different to that of the others, so bolt upright and so stiff, you know, just as if he was a soldier; but he is not so devout as the others."

"He has a profound knowledge of the Talmud, as in the course of this very day I became aware, and I'm glad of that--you know I take no rent from our lodger, only make a point of having a god-fearing sound Talmudist in the house; but tell me, dear wife, what makes you think that he holds himself like a soldier?"

"Nay, because they hold themselves straight and upright. What is there remarkable in that."

"Nothing, nothing,--but I have not yet told you; yesterday evening, when I came home from the midnight-prayer-meeting, just as I was going to unlock the door of our cottage--I always take the key with me that I may not be obliged to wake you--I heard a loud voice in our lodger's room; I listened a moment.--It was not the way, in which one studies the Talmud--he seemed to be addressing one or more persons, but what he said had such a strange ring about it, I could not at first clearly make it out, especially as according to the tenor of his words he at one moment muttered softly, at another cried loud out--the wind moreover whistled loud through the passage; but my ear soon grew accustomed to the sound, and I heard him plainly say: 'Man, we are both lost--both of us, you and I--they will betray us to the Imperialists--they will deliver us to our deadliest enemy,' afterwards he cried out again suddenly--'they shall not surprise us! we are armed, march, halt! fire! storm! no quarter--they give none, level everything. Ah, ah, blood, blood! that refreshes the soul. The victory is mine! mine the blood stained laurel wreath, I am victor,--I victor. Ah me, it avails nothing, I am still a ----' the last words died lightly away. After some minutes all was again still in the room, and I heard the measured breathing of his mighty breast. This is the first opportunity that I have had of telling you about it, for Friday, as you know, I am entirely occupied by my duty in the synagogue,--I might, perhaps, have forgotten it, had not you remarked upon his military aspect."--

"I am not at all surprised that he has such dreams," replied Schöndel, "his mind is always full of such wonderful things.--This morning, when I wanted to fetch for you your Sabbath clothes out of the chest, that he lets us leave in his room, getting no answer to my knock, I lifted up the latch, to assure myself that he was out; but the door came open and Gabriel, his head resting on both hands, was gazing with fixed attention--not on a folio, but a roll of coloured paper on which he was drawing different lines with a pen. When I got nearer, I made out that it was a map. I asked him in astonishment what that meant, and he told me that as he travelled from Germany to Prague, he had in the course of his journey encountered the Bohemian and Imperial armies, and that to amuse himself he was now looking where they were--then he pointed out to me the exact spot, where the brave Field-Marshal Mannsfield was, where the Elector Maximilian, and Generals Tilly and Boucquoi lay with their troops, then he showed me how badly Christian of Anhalt, Frederick's General-in-chief, was supporting the operations of the brave Ernest of Mannsfield, and how that the troops of the union in spite of their bravery and gallant leader must succumb, so long as Anhalt, incapable, or as he expressed himself, perhaps won over by the Imperialists remained at the head of the army: all this he explained to me so clearly, and distinctly, that even I, a foolish woman, could quite easily see the force of it.--'How do you come to have such a clear perception of all that,' I enquired, 'of all the students of the present School not one would understand so much about these things as you--you'd make a good officer.' 'Nay, who knows,' he laughingly answered, 'if some day I do not get a good Rabbinate, I may still become a soldier.' The whole occurrence struck me as so strange, that it haunted me the whole day; I cannot help smiling when I think of it. In the middle of the day, about three hours afterwards, as I crossed over to the 'Kleinseite' to buy some wax tapers, I saw two superior officers riding over the bridge, one I happened to know, the young Thurn--every child here knows him; but as to the other, a captain, who rode a perfectly black horse, he seemed to me as like our lodger Gabriel, as one twin-brother is to the other, and as they both turned the corner into the 'Kleinseite,' this captain caught sight of me and gave me such a friendly unconstrained look, as if he would greet me. But all this was a pure deception, the whole resemblance may have been a slight and casual one, and Gabriel's strange conversation of which my thoughts were still full, may have probably been the cause of my exaggerating the likeness--and that officers turn round to stare at young women, is certainly no new occurrence."

"Trust me," answered Schlome, "Gabriel is no captain. The students of the School at Prague are not the stuff out of which kings, or states would fashion heroes. I do not say that they would not make as good as others.--The Maccabees fought as bravely as a Thurn, a Boucquoi, a Mannsfield, and even more bravely,--but so long as the Lord of Hosts in his lofty wisdom does not entirely turn the hearts of the princes and peoples among whom we live, we must accept oppression, contumely, scorn, and all else that Providence has ordained for us. Do you not know, that for some years the fencing-masters here in Prague have been forbidden to teach the Jews the noble art of fencing? But, dear wife, this is no pleasant subject of conversation for a joyful Friday-evening."

"You are ungrateful! Do we not now live quietly under the protection of the laws? Look back to the dark and horrible times of yore."--

"To-day let us conjure up no sad memories, let us not disturb a joyous Sabbath peace," implored Schlome, "let us speak of something else, of what you will. You say our lodger is not as devout as other students?"

"No, he is not so industrious, does not often attend a lecture on the Talmud, even in the few days that he has been here has often neglected to attend at synagogue; besides he never kisses the scroll on the door as he goes in and out."

Schlome was about to answer, but was prevented by the hurried entrance of Gabriel, who by an actual omission confirmed the assertion that had just been made.

"A happy Sabbath to you; excuse my late return. I was in the old New-synagogue, an awe striking synagogue! We hear much of this synagogue in my country. It is certainly one of the most ancient Judaic buildings in Europe, if we except the house of God at Worms, perhaps, the most ancient;--but tell me, good man, are all the stories, that they tell us in the schools of Germany, especially towards midnight, about this edifice and which have often caused me a thrill of pleasant ghostly horror, true?"

"The child-like temper of the people," replied the goodman, "delight in the unwonted and strange, and then many stories are told, that in reality may have happened very differently."

"Yes, but there is much truth in it," interposed the good wife; "ah, this community of Prague has in the course of time met with so much sorrow, has suffered such endless anguish, and yet God--blessed be his name--has so wonderfully supported it, that even now it shines forth a brilliant example to its sisters in Germany. Whenever I pass that ancient and reverend house of God, pictures of the days that are gone come back upon me. Do you know the history of how our brethren in the faith were once ruthlessly slaughtered in the old New-synagogue?"

Schöndel was obliged to repeat this question; Gabriel seemed suddenly lost in deep reflection. "No," said he, at length arousing himself from his reveries, as though his spirit was for away;--"tell it, noble lady! Everything sounds doubly beautiful from your rosy lips."--

Schlome shook his head in thoughtful astonishment over this manner of speaking, so different from that usual with Talmud-students.

"Reb Gabriel! you talk like a knight to a lady of rank. Do not forget that you are a student of the Talmud, and my wife the wife of a servant."

"You must not talk as if you wished to mock us," said Schöndel, and a deep flush suffused her face; "or I cannot"--

"Oh, the story, good wife! mind not my talk. I am at times absent, and often far off in imagination."

"High on horseback in the battle, is it not so?" asked Schöndel slily.

The face of the student became a deep dark red. He required a moment to recover command of himself. "What do you mean by that?" he impetuously demanded.

"Women are gossiping, as you know from the Talmud and surely from your own experience also," said Schlome. "I was just telling my wife, as we waited for you, that yesterday when I returned from midnight prayer, as I passed by the door of your room, I could hear you call out loud in your sleep, and that you appeared to be dreaming of a battle or something of that kind.--We thought the dream a strange one for a student."

"Ah," said Gabriel, drawing a deep breath, and visibly relieved--"ah, you thought so? Well, I do sometimes dream heavily of battles.--But do you know, how that happens? I was too industrious as a student--studied the Talmud day and night; but a man cannot endure too much work, and as my ambition compelled me to unbroken exertion, it fell out, that my mind became confused, I became subject to delusions and fancied myself, a knight, a warrior--but I am now thanks to a clever physician and rest of body and mind, perfectly well again, perfectly! Do not be anxious!--But as on my journey here I encountered many troops of soldiers, my mind may again in sleep have been terrified by gloomy visions: for although I am now quite well, yet still, if I have shortly before been excited about anything, unpleasant dreams are wont to pain me; but they are only dreams; and it seldom happens, so I beg you to pay no attention if I do again talk such strange stuff in my sleep."

It was an age, when the study of the Talmud afforded almost the only outlet for spiritual activity. It was no uncommon event for a student, especially if he combined an ascetic life with hard study, to unhinge his mind by what is called over-study. It was known too, that mental derangements which had been caused in that way, could be healed by sensible treatment, rest of body and mind, just as Gabriel had stated, and the husband and wife themselves knew more than one student, who had been affected just in the same way as their lodger, and like him too had recovered. They had no reason, therefore, for doubting Gabriel's open confession, and even the obvious embarrassment, that he had evinced at the quick retort of the good-wife seemed entirely justified by the really unpleasant and affecting confession that had been wrung from him.

"Poor young man," thus Schöndel broke the long pause that intervened and began to be uncomfortable. "Thank God,--praised be he therefore!--that he hath helped you, and be right glad. Now I too understand, wherefore you took such warm sympathy in the old Jacob, and immediately granted his request."

"No, that was not the reason," said Gabriel earnestly, and reflectively, as if in fact he too participated in Schöndel's wonder, and could find within himself no sufficient explanation of his behaviour at that time--"but please, let us leave this subject, and talk of something else.--You were going to tell me, how once on a time."

"Yes, yes," cried Schöndel, glad to be able to give another direction to the conversation; "listen: It must be now more than two hundred years ago,--Wenceslaus the *Slothful* was ruler of the country--when it fell out that a knight was inflamed with a hot lust for a Jewish maiden. She rejected his shameful proposals with virtuous indignation. Cunning and seductive arts were shattered against the maiden's steadfast determination. The knight, therefore, resolved to attain his warmly coveted aim by violence. The day of the feast of the atonement seemed to him the best suited for the accomplishment of his ruthless plan. He knew, that Judith--so the maiden was named--would on that day stay at home alone with her blind mother, while all the rest were detained by prayer and devout exercises in the house of God. On the evening of that day--Judith was softly praying by the bed-side of her slumbering mother--the door of her chamber opened, and her detested persecutor entered with sparkling eager look. Unmoved by the prayers, the tears of Judith, he already held her fast embraced in his powerful arms when a lucky chance brought home her brother to enquire after the health of his mother and sister. The terrible unutterable wrath that took possession of him, gave the man, naturally powerful, the strength of a giant. He wrenched his arms from the villain, who had only the women to thank, that he did not by the forfeit of his life pay for the attempted infamy. With kicks and grim mockery the outraged brother expelled the dissolute fellow from the house. The knight given over to the scorn of the people who had assembled in considerable numbers, swore a bloody deadly revenge against the Jews. He kept his word--Reb Gabriel! for God's sake! what is the matter with you?" suddenly the narrator interrupted herself; "are you unwell?"

Gabriel, who had listened to the housewife, with ever growing attention, was in fact at this moment a sight to look upon, his features had become as pale as ashes and twitched convulsively, his large and glassy eyes were fixed immoveably on one spot, as though he saw a ghost.

"What ails you?" cried Schlome, shaking his lodger with all his force, "recover yourself."

Gabriel's lips closed more than once with a quiver, without being able to give forth an intelligible sound; at length he passed his hand across his forehead that was covered with a cold sweat, and said with a powerful effort at self-command, and as if awaking from a dream: "That was in the days of King Wenceslaus, was it not? two hundred years ago,--a blind mother--a beautiful daughter--and the day of reconciliation was it?"

"Thank God, that you are well again, you must have had a sudden giddiness."

"Yes, yes," said Gabriel, faint and enfeebled, "I felt very unwell for a moment, very unwell--but I am better again. Go on with your story, dear lady, I pray you, go on with it."

Complying with his urgent request, Schöndel continued: "Long ago expelled from the ranks of the nobility on account of his worthless behaviour, the knight had cultivated a connection with some discontented idle burghers of the city, and these he hoped to make the ministers of his cruel vengeance. Some short time afterward he put himself at the head of a mob rendered fanatical under frivolous pretexts to murder and plunder in the Jews-town. The first, who, frightened out of their peaceful dwellings, went to meet the robbers, were cut down. Determined men endeavoured to oppose a monstrously superior force. Vain effort. Without arms, they saw themselves after an heroic opposition compelled to take refuge in the old New-synagogue already filled with old men, women, and children. Mighty blows sounded heavily on the closed doors of the synagogue. 'Open and give yourselves up,' yelled the knight from outside. After a short pause of consultation answer was made, that the Jews would deliver their property over to the mutineers, would draw up a deed of gift of it, and only keep back for themselves absolute necessaries; they also promised to make no complaint to king or states, in exchange for which, the honour of their wives and daughters was to be preserved, and no one compelled to change his religion.

"'It is not your business,' a voice from outside again resounded, 'it is ours to dictate conditions.--Do you desire life and not a wretched death, then open and at once abjure your faith. I grant but short delay for reflection; if that fruitlessly elapses, you are one and all given over to death!'

"No answer followed. Farther resistance could not be thought of, and hope that the king would at length put a stop to this unheard of, unparalleled iniquity, grew every moment less. The battle in the street--if the desperate resistance of a few unarmed men against an armed superior force could be called by that name--had lasted so long; that King Wenceslaus might have easily sent assistance; but none came. They were at length constrained to admit, that he did not trouble himself about the fate of the Jews. A silence as of death reigned in the synagogue; only here and there a suppressed sobbing, only here and there an infant at the breast, that reminded its mother of her sweetest duty, was heard. Once more the voice of the knight thundered rough and wild: 'I demand of you for the last time, whether do you choose: the new faith or death?' There was a momentary silence, then broke a cry of thousands 'Death' with a dull sound against the roof of the house that was consecrated to God.--The insurgents now began to demolish the doors with axes and hatchets. But the besieged in their deadly agony lifted up their voice in wonderful accord, and sang in solemn chorus the glorious verse of the Psalmist:

'Though I walk through the valley of the shadow of death
I will not fear the crafty wiliness of the evil-doer
For thou art with me! Thou art in all my ways:
The firm staff of faith is my confidence!'

"The aged Rabbi had sunk upon his knees in prayer upon the steps that led up to the tabernacle. 'Lord,' he implored, 'I suffer infinite sorrow, yet, oh that we might fall into the hands of the Lord, for his mercy is boundless.--Only not into the hand of man! Ah, we know not what to do; to Thee alone we look for succour! Call to remembrance Thy mercy and gracious favour, that has been ever of old. In anger be mindful of compassion! Let Thy goodness be showed unto us, as we do put our trust in Thee!'

"But God at this season did not succour his children, in his unsearchable counsels it was otherwise ordered. The first door was burst open, the mob pressed into the vestibule of God's house, a single frail door separated oppressed and oppressors.

"'Lord,' cried the Rabbi in accents of deepest despair, 'Lord, grant that the walls of this house in which we and our fathers with songs of praise have glorified and blessed Thy name--that the walls of this temple of God may fall together, and that we may find a grave under its ruins! But let us not fall alive into the hands of the barbarians, let not our wives and maidens become a living prey to the wicked.' 'No,' now exclaimed a powerful voice, 'that shall they not, Rabbi!--Wives and maidens; do you prefer death at the hand of your fathers, husbands, brothers, death at your own hands to shame and dishonour? Would you appear pure and innocent before the throne of the Almighty instead of falling living victims into the hands of those blood-thirsty inhuman men outside.--Would you? Speak, time presses,' and again resounded from a hundred women's lips 'Rather death than dishonour!'--

"His lovely blooming wife pressed up close to the side of the man who had thus spoken, her baby at her breast: 'Let me be the first, let me receive my death from thy loved hands,' she murmured softly. With the deepest emotion of which a human soul is capable he clasped her to his breast. 'It must be done quickly,' he said with hollow trembling voice. 'The separation must be speedy, I never thought to part from you thus! Lord, Most Merciful, forgive us, we do it for Thy holy name's sake alone! Art thou ready?'

"'I am,' she said, 'let me only once more, but once more, for the last time kiss my sweet, my innocent child--God bless thee, poor orphan, God suffer thee to find compassion in the eyes of our murderers.... God help thee! We, dear friend, we part but for a short time, thou wilt follow me soon, thou true-hearted!'--

"With the most infinite sorrow that can thrill a human breast, the husband pressed a fervent parting kiss, and a last touch of the hand upon the loved infant that absolutely refused to leave its mother, and the bared and heaving breast.--One stroke of the knife, and a jet of blood sprinkled the child's face and spouted up against the walls of the house of God.--The woman sank, with a cry of 'Hear, o Israel, the Everlasting our God is God alone' and fell lifeless on her knees.--

"All the other women, including Judith, followed the heroically courageous example. Many died by their own hands, many received the death-stroke from their husbands, fathers, brothers, but all of them without a murmur, silent and resigned to God's will. They had to tear away tender children, who weeping and wringing their hands climbed on to their father's knees, and piteously implored them, not to hurt their mother--it was a scene, horrible and heart-rending, a scene than which the history of the Jews, the history of mankind knows none more agonising. It was accomplished! No woman might fall alive into the hands of the persecutors, the last death-sigh was breathed, and the few stout men, who had desired only so long to defend the inner door, stepped backward. A fearful blow, and the door, the last bulwark, fell in, sending clouds of dust whirling over it. The knight, brandished battle-axe in hand, stood on the steps that led up into the house of prayer, his countenance disfigured by wrath, behind him crowded an immeasurable mass of people armed with spits and clubs and iron flails. 'Yield your women and children,' he shouted in a voice of thunder, at length betraying his real intention--'and abjure your faith!'

"'Look at these blood-dripping steaming corpses,' said a man who stood nearest the door, 'they are women and maidens, they have all preferred death to dishonour.--Do you think that we men fear death at thy hands and the hands of thy murderous associates? Murder me, monster, and be accursed, here and hereafter, in this world and the next, for ever and ever!'--a moment afterwards the bold speaker lay on the ground weltering in his blood. At sight of the countless corpses of the women the beastly rage of the populace, that saw itself cheated of the fairest portion of its booty, mounted to absolute madness. Hyenas drunk with blood would have behaved with greater humanity. Not a life was spared, and even infants were slaughtered over the bodies of their mothers. Blood flowed in streams. One boy alone was later on dragged still living from under the heaps of dead. As they approached the tabernacle, in order to inflict the death-stroke on the Rabbi, who knelt on the steps before it, they found him lifeless, his head turned upwards towards the East, a soft smile upon his death-like features. Death had anticipated them; his pure soul had exhaled in fervent prayer.

"The mob surveyed the work that had been accomplished, and now that the thirst for blood was stilled, shrunk in terror before the bloody horror that had been perpetrated.--The tabernacle remained untouched, the house of God unplundered. Discharging oaths and curses at the knight, their ringleader, the wild troop dispersed in apprehensive fright of the divine and human judge. But King Wenceslaus left the iniquity, in spite of the most urgent representations of the Bohemian nobility, unvisited and unpunished. But from that day his good angel left him. The spirit of those helpless murdered ones seemed continually to hover about his head. His reign became unfortunate. The nobility felt itself deeply injured by this outrage upon justice. A series of interminable disputes sprung up between the nobles and populace, and Wenceslaus who went on from one cruelty to another was twice imprisoned by the states, and died at length, probably of the trouble and anxiety cause by a bloody revolt of the Hussites that had broken out shortly before his death. To his life's end he never recovered either happiness on confidence.--The knight too, the author of that foul deed, who afterwards marched through the country, burning, robbing and murdering was overtaken by a righteous punishment. The Archbishop of Prague ten years later, at the time of the second captivity of Wenceslaus, hanged him up with fifty other robbers in sight of the city of Prague.--His name was forgotten."

"You are a wonderful narrator," thus Gabriel broke the silence that had lasted for some time, after Schöndel had ended her story: "I could listen to you by the hour."

Indeed he had been especially struck by the impassioned elevation of her language, and the choiceness of her expressions so little in accordance with her position in life.

"Excuse a question," he began again after a short pause. "I feel myself for the first time really at home, when I am intimately acquainted with those about me. A happy chance led me to your house, a house than which I could not wish or find a better--but you will not be offended with my frankness.

I am surprised to find such remarkably easy circumstances in the house of a servant, and still more in you, dear goodwife, such an unusually high degree of cultivation.--Perhaps, you will explain this to me."

"Oh yes," replied the goodman, "but at table, it is late and we will sup."

The three took their seats and an old maidservant came in. The goodman said a blessing over a flagon of wine, they washed their hands, and after grace had been said over two cakes of white bread that had up to that moment been covered by a velvet cloth, the maid-servant placed the smoking dishes on the table. The two men set too with a will.

"You know, Reb Gabriel," began Schlome, "where two are sitting and the word of God is not between them so may I ask you to impart to me some of the results of your religious researches."

"Researches," said Gabriel slowly, "I will try"--and passing his hands slowly over his forehead, and rubbing his eyes as though he would force back all other thoughts, and conjure up recollections long left in the background, he began a very ingenious dissertation upon the Talmud. At first measured and thoughtful as though moving on strange and slippery ground, he became gradually more confident and at home, and expressed himself as he warmed with that oriental vivacity, that gives to these studies a singular attraction. He displayed unusual knowledge. All that he said, was so acutely considered and well-balanced, that he easily repelled the objections that Reb Schlome here and there attempted to interpose. He, in spite of his ripe knowledge of the Talmud and his practised dexterity soon saw the futility of every disputation and listened to the student in almost reverential silence to the end. "That is a glorious dissertation," he said, when Gabriel left off speaking, "and our assessor of the college of Rabbis, Reb. Lippman Heller will be delighted to have got such a scholar. But you do not often attend his lectures?"

"I have as yet had a good deal to arrange after my journey and cannot attend the lecture as often as I could wish; but now, dear sir, as we have already had our discourse on the Talmud, tell me, how it happens that you are so prosperous and yet a servant, how it comes to pass that your wife has attained to such a high degree of culture, as one so seldom finds in a Jew, especially a woman, on account of the oppression that the Jews, in spite of much even if slow progress, have still to endure. Explain this to me, unless special reasons impose silence upon you."

Schlome, who had already enjoyed the thought of proving to his guest that he too had profitably devoted himself to Talmudic studies, was obliged to put it off to another opportunity and yield to the earnestly expressed wish of his guest. "I am now much pleased with you, Reb Gabriel, and as I feel more and more convinced that you are a genuine scholar, a certain feeling of distrust--I may now confess it openly--that sometimes came over me with respect to you, is disappearing, and I am heartily rejoiced at these your frank expressions.--So listen: I am the son of Reb Carpel Sachs--may the memory of the just be blessed.--My father was a very rich and pious man and made the best use of his fortune. The Community, whose chief overseer, and the Old-synagogue, whose ruler he was, have much to be thankful to him for. I was his only child and was the more precious to my father, as in me the memory of my early lost mother survived to him. His affectionate care for me knew no bounds. I never dared to go out alone, I never dared to leave him even for a moment, and all my tutors were obliged to give me their lessons in his presence. As overseer of the community frequently brought into relation with the leading men of other religions, he saw the necessity of a Jew, devoting himself to the assiduous study of universal sciences as well as to more strictly religious studies, that the Jewish nation might stand worthily by the side of the whole race of mankind as opposed to the Judaic alone. In spite of his many occupations he was often with the worthy Löwe, and the partner of his varied studies. I myself very early received instruction in the learned languages and natural science, without on that account at all neglecting the study of our holy scripture. It was on a lovely winter morning, I, a little boy, was sitting by my father in his study reading the Bible. The servant announced a man, who urgently desired to see my father, and almost immediately he entered the room carrying a little girl in his arms. I shall never forget the scene, even this day it rises up before me clear and lifelike.--The man was large and strongly built, but deep lines of sorrow and trouble were stamped upon his earnest noble features. The child, that with anxious tenderness he still held in his arms, was a lovely blooming little girl; I need not farther describe her, picture to yourself my goodwife, a girl of three year's old. Both were poorly clothed, the stranger wore the dress of a needy wandering Pole, the little girl seemed insufficiently protected from the cold by her tattered garments, and her father--for that the stranger apparently was--warmed her tiny frozen hands that were fast entwined round his neck with the breath of his mouth.

"'I and my child,' said the stranger, 'arrive from a long and difficult journey. I have come straight to your house, Reb Carpel, I ask that help from you, that you both can and will afford me. Grant me an hour of your time, I must speak with you alone.' These few words of the stranger, and even before they had been spoken, his reverend aspect had obviously, in spite of the meanness of his dress, made a favourable impression upon my father. He rose from his seat, held out his hand to his visitor in sign of welcome, and placed a chair by the stove in which an hospitable fire was burning. My father bid me take the little girl with me to my room, and let the servant give her some supper. Schöndel looked at her father, and when he put her down, and told her she might, took hold of my hand with a confiding smile and went with me, I do not know what passed in secret between the two men, but when two hours later my father opened the door of his apartment, I heard him say aloud: 'Since you will neither be our counsellor nor assessor, nor Klaus Rabbi, I consider it a special Providence, that just at this very moment the post of upper-attendant in the Old-synagogue is vacant, that that exactly meets your wishes, that I can have a decisive word in arranging your appointment. I believe that I am sure of the consent of my associates. I will see besides that that respect, Rabbi, which is your due, is paid to you by all the servants and the congregation, with whom in truth you will not be brought into contact. You will be able to live in the manner you wish, unknown, cut off from all society, devoted to your studies. I look upon it as a piece of good fortune, Rabbi, that you have granted my request, and consent to initiate my boy in the depths of our holy Scripture.' 'I thank thee, Reb Carpel, but call me not Rabbi, call me Mosche as....' He saw me and stopped.

"I was astounded at the almost reverential behaviour of my father. The first person in the community, he well knew how to keep up his dignity on all occasions, and it could only be a very distinguished individual indeed, who could be gladdened by such treatment.

"'Schlome, kiss the Rabbi's hand, from to-day he will undertake the care of your education,' said my father. I lifted his hand respectfully to my lips and from that time Reb Mosche seemed to me a being of a superior nature. My father let him immediately into occupation of a house close to the synagogue, the residence of the upper-attendant for the time being, the very rooms in which we are now living, and the next Saturday, after a long parley with the other overseers of the synagogue, it was announced to the frequenters of the Old-synagogue, that a stranger, for whom Reb Carpel Sachs answered in every respect, had been appointed upper-attendant. Here then my step-father lived, here it was that I as little boy came to make my first essay in the study of the Talmud, here we closed his wearied eyes. Rabbi Mosche was a wonderful man, all that, he said and did evinced the profoundest religious feeling. He lived retired from all society and the only visits that he received were from the high Rabbi Löwe and my father. His expositions were clear and easy to be understood, and my rapt attention, and firm determination to win his approbation came excellently to the aid of my lessons. The man usually so reserved, soon shared his love between his only child, whom he almost idolised, and me. My father too loved with an infinite love the stranger's motherless child. We children clung to one another with extraordinary tenderness, a feeling, that, God be praised and thanked, has never been extinguished in our hearts. When I received nay lessons from her revered father, Schöndel would sit by me by the hour and listen, and even when I was occupied by other studies, the dear little maid was my constant companion. To this circumstance and to the remarkable industry and talents of my wife you must ascribe the fact, that in a menial position she surpasses in knowledge and culture many ladies of rank.--In a word, this confined room was even in my free hours the place where I loved best to be, I knew no higher enjoyment than to converse with Rabbi Mosche. I was often allowed to help him in certain business about the synagogue, and I was the more glad to do so, as it enabled him to decline the assistance of all the inferior servants that were under his orders. What a childish pleasure I took on every Thursday evening at the thought of the coming morning! Friday, I was always up betimes, no need to wake me--dressed myself and ran down to Reb Mosche. He was already expecting me, I took his hand and we went together to the adjoining house of God. To this day a perfectly empty temple makes a singular, not easily to be described impression upon me, and when the grating doors opened and our steps echoed loud in the cool and empty space, it seemed to me as though the blissful breath of God's peace was upon me. My teacher first opened his desk in the tribune, then placed candles in the chandeliers, and trimmed the lamp, that ever burneth, with fresh oil, and I was allowed to follow him carrying the flask of oil, candles and everything that he usually wanted. All this was done in the profoundest silence, as if we feared by a word to dispel the stillness that reigned through the building dedicated to God's service. When all was duly arranged I sat me down on the steps that led up to the tabernacle and began to read out of the Bible to my teacher the portions of Scripture appointed for the week. The earliest frequenters of the synagogue found us ever busy with our studies in the Bible. I passed a peaceful and contented youth. The mysterious obscurity that enveloped my second father,--for so had Reb Mosche become to me--was only calculated to heighten, if possible, the feeling of reverence with which he had inspired me and I dared not even wish to raise this veil that enshrouded him. Neither Schöndel nor I would for worlds have asked him about his past life, which had of a surety been fruitful of sorrow to him, and even my father, to whom his secret was probably known, preserved the most unbroken silence with respect to it. The mutual relation of the two men was also a singular one. Sometimes they addressed one another, as though years and years ago they had known one another as children, and yet my father had never left his native town, while Reb Mosche on the contrary--Schöndel could just remember it as in a dream--had come from a very great way off. I myself with respect to Reb Mosche adopted that demeanour which the Talmud enjoins in the intercourse of scholar and tutor. I fulfilled his smallest wishes, and learned to interpret them from his look; and if I chanced without intending it to vex him by my talk, I was inconsolable and could have wept by the hour. This, however, seldom happened, and I can only recollect one instance of it. As we were reading the Psalms we had come to that passage, 'Behold how good and how pleasant it is for brethren to dwell together in unity!' and I expressed the childish wish, that as well as Schöndel whom I regarded as my dear little sister, I had a brother too. 'My son,' replied Reb Mosche earnestly, 'what God doeth, that is well done! Wherefore dost thou desire a brother? Brothers do not always love one another, there where love and friendship should prevail, enmity and strife have often mastery. Cain slew his brother Abel, Jacob and Esau were brothers, but Esau hated Jacob. Joseph was sold by his brethren, and the brethren of the greatest prophet, even the brethren of Moses spoke evil of him.' I gazed in astonishment at the face of my respected teacher, a bitter smile played upon his lips, a tear shone in his mild eye.--

"I will not further weary you with the descriptions of my youth,--which while they fill me with sad remembrances, are probably to you a matter of indifference. My youth slipped away as happily and as untroubled as my childhood. I ripened to manhood, Schöndel developed into a most beautiful young woman. Our infelt mutual attachment was known to both fathers, and Schöndel's two and twentieth birthday was fixed for our betrothal.--Eight days before, one Saturday afternoon I was sent for to the room of my father, where I found my father-in-law also. 'My son,' he began, with deep emotion, 'I have joyfully consented to your marriage, I have known you from a child, you are infinitely beloved and dear to me, and I can now depart in peace from my own loved child whenever the Lord calls me. But I have a request to make to you, and your own worthy father adds his prayers to mine. See, Schlome, see, I have early grown grey with trouble and sorrow, I have been unhappy, and to-day I must confess it to you with deepest affliction, have learned to know the iniquity of mankind. We both, thy father and I, are ignorant when God will send his messenger to us.--Schlome, do not refuse our request! *Remain always attendant in the synagogue*." I was for a moment petrified with astonishment, I had expected anything but this wish; but it was not for me to pry into the reasons of the strange petition. My father fully agreed with him, I had nothing to do but consent.--Eight days afterwards was the wedding. The poor of the community had liberal alms, every synagogue, every charitable institution was bountifully remembered, but the marriage-feast was celebrated quietly and without display. When the two fathers came home from the wedding, they fell into one another's arms with expressions of the highest excitement, 'Reb. Carpel! could you have hoped for this when we separated forty years ago,' asked my father-in-law, 'could we have expected ever to meet again? and yet the gracious Lord of all grants us the felicity of uniting our only loved children in the holy bonds of wedlock.' 'Now, we may die in peace,' replied my father, with the deepest emotion.

"My father seemed to have spoken prophetically. In the first year of our marriage died my never-to-be-forgotten father, shortly afterwards my father-in-law. Their souls seemed linked to one another by the bonds of friendship even for the next world, and they rest in adjoining graves.

"'My children,' said Rabbi Mosche, on his deathbed, 'your father, Reb. Carpel Sachs, has left you a store of this world's goods, I am poor, I leave you naught but my blessing, my infinite love. In this sealed packet is the record of my life's history written in the long winter nights for your benefit. Only after twenty years may you break the seal, when he that wished to do me evil, is dead, and God will have already forgiven him. That which was dark to you will then become clear. My life was dedicated first to God, next to you, and my boundless love will not expire with my last breath. Have God ever before your eyes, what he doeth that he doeth well. This world is but the vestibule of a more beauteous world beyond. Murmur not. Trust in God! Farewell! God bless you. May the Eternal One let the light of his countenance shine upon you. May the Everlasting turn his face upon you and give you peace for evermore! Hear, o Israel, the Everlasting our God is one God!' that was his last breath, his beautiful soul expired."

Reb Schlome was obliged to stop, the recollection had seized him with overpowering might, his wife too sobbed aloud.

"We had suffered two violent blows following quickly one upon the other," he continued after a long pause with more composure. "The unutterable grief that filled us can only be measured by one whose bosom has felt a like affliction, who has stood at the death-bed of a man, as highly prized and dear to him. We felt as if the whole world had escaped our grasp, we both were now so solitary and forsaken."

"Solitary and forsaken," echoed Gabriel in a heart-rending voice that quivered with agony, "solitary and forsaken, and yet ye were two, who hung upon one another with infinite affection."

"You too have stood sorrowing, solitary and forsaken, by the bed of a dying father, a dying mother?" asked Schöndel with infelt sympathy.

"Yes, yes," replied Gabriel vehemently, almost screaming. "Yes, yes, I did once stand by a mother's death-bed, wringing my hands and despairing!

Oh, a very tender mother, virtuous and tender, she loved me, her only child, with a love that conquered death.--Oh, a good, good mother, and I was, indeed, *solitary and forsaken when she died*!"

The student spoke these words with wild and passionate bitterness, his large and brilliant eyes rolled restlessly, a pallor as of death, and a purple flush covered in rapid succession his face marred, but once so beautiful.

"Do not let the recollection obtain such mastery over you," implored Schöndel soothingly, "consider: Perchance you have still a tender father."--

"A tender father? No--yes.--Is it not true, fathers are all tender, more tender than mothers?--

"Neither husband or wife had ever known a mother and kept silence."

"A father!" repeated Gabriel, with an expression of the most poignant despair, and as though he would force back the overflowing tide of his feelings, he pressed his hands violently against his breast; and then after a short pause recovered himself, wiped the sweat, that had collected in heavy drops, from his forehead and said with a visible effort, "Excuse me, my friends, but you know, profound sorrow cannot be restrained."

"Your sorrow must still be fresh," remarked Schlome.

"Oh, a deep heart-wound is never healed. But enough of this, proceed," exclaimed Gabriel; "the twenty years have not yet elapsed, and you are still unacquainted with the affecting fortunes of your father-in-law?"

"No, it is but nine years since he passed into a more beautiful existence, his life-history still rests unopened in the chest that stands in your room.--We do not even know the name of his family."

"Strange!" said Gabriel; "you too never knew your mother? dear housewife."--

"My father never alluded to his past history," she replied, "my mother must have died in my earliest childhood."--

"Well for you!" cried Gabriel, and as both gazed at him in astonishment, he continued hurriedly, "Well for you, that you cleave to your father with the indissoluble link of love, that he still survives in your memory; may you some day thus survive in the heart of your--but you have no children?"

"God has not blessed our union with children," answered Schöndel, sadly.

"What God doeth, is well done! cling fast to that belief," now interposed Schlome, in quiet and earnest accents. "See, I was once sore troubled about it; we, my wife and I, have neither brethren, nor friends--we always lived so retired from all company--and even if we had friends, the love of a child for its parents can be supplied by nothing else, nothing can be weighed in the balance with it.... It made me sad when I thought that if the Lord should call me or my wife to himself, one of us must be left behind, desolate and forsaken in bitterest woe.--It made me sad when I thought, that with us would be entombed the memory of my father and father-in-law, that with me the long web would be broken, that humanity was ever destined to weave since the world's creation.--But consoling encouraging thoughts in time germinated in my heart. 'Murmur not! this world is but a vestibule of the next,' had my father said, and says not also the prophet? 'Oh, let not the childless lament, I am as grass that withereth!--Thus saith the Lord to them that are childless, they that observe my feast-days, and choose that which pleaseth me and hold fast to my covenant. Even unto them will I give in my house and within my walls a place, and a name better than of sons and of daughters. I will give them an everlasting name that shall not be cut off.' I bow to the decree of the Allwise, what he doeth is well done--I live happy in the performance of my duties, for the future, One that is above will provide--if, hereafter, my soulless body be lowered by strangers into the vault, my spirit will mount upwards to God!"--

Schlome spoke with honest warmth, this was no pleasant self-deception, it was his clear, mature, and veritable intuition. When he had ended, a pause ensued. The oil-lamps began to go out one by one, and Schöndel remarked, that grace had not yet been said. A quarter of an hour afterwards Gabriel took his leave and retired to his room. Here the careful housewife even before the break of the Sabbath had lit a well-filled lamp, that still burned clear. Gabriel shut the door rapidly and tossing off cloak and cap, cried with gnashing teeth and fists spasmodically clenched, "Tear pitilessly at the ever bleeding wounds of my heart, keen was your aim and sure the blow, you could not have rent my raging soul with a pang of greater anguish! Did you gaze into the secrets of my breast? Is a Cain's sign imprinted on my forehead, that every one at his will may read upon it my ignominious past? As this woman with flashing eyes spoke to me of that day of atonement, of that knight, of that Jewish maiden and her blind mother--and how they cast him forth with mockery and scorn--did it not seem as if she would have unfolded before me a detested period of my own life? And when she looked at me and asked if I had ever stood solitary and forsaken by the death-bed of a mother? If I had yet a tender father? that was no chance, that cannot have been a chance.--Chance can decide battles. Chance can let me fall alive into the hands of the Imperialists--but that is no chance, that is a presentiment, a dark impulse, an instinct, to hate me, to mortify me. But you are right, I hate you too, with the most unbridled strength of a sore, provoked tiger-

-revenge, to revenge myself, that is now the only thought that keeps me alive.--I must find the woman, the *woman,* that might have saved me as I hovered on the brink of a bottomless abyss--and that let me be dashed to pieces--I must find her, she cannot escape me--she is here in Prague, shut up within the gates of the Ghetto! Oh, how I gloat upon a sweet revenge--to take sweet and fearful vengeance, and then to perish for ever.--But what if I should die first, if the trumpet summoned me to battle, if I perished on the field,--if the outlaw fell alive into the hands of the Imperialists! No, no, that cannot be or--there is in sooth a God."

Gabriel paced his chamber impetuously--visions of the past filling him with the most torturing recollections, passed over his soul.--To die? He said at length suddenly stopping, "I fear not death, I have looked it in the face motionless and unconcerned in the whirl of battle, but before I die, oh, that I might find him, whom I have sought for ten long years, whom I might, perhaps, even yet embrace in these arms.--Thou, whom men call all-mighty and all-merciful," he suddenly cried, opening the window and lifting his gaze to the starry heaven, "Thou! give me my father, give me him though it be at my life's last breath--let him rest one moment, and may it be my last, on my breast--and I will acknowledge Thee, and I will bend my proud spirit even in death before Thee! But where to seek him, where to find him! I am sure of nothing, am sure of nothing but that I hate them all with a nameless hatred, and have good reason to hate them!"--

Chapter III

On Saturday Gabriel had gone to early prayers with his landlord in the Old-synagogue. The service had lasted till near mid-day. Reb Schlome had then paid a visit to the chief Rabbi. At the midday meal, which was shared by two guests, they met again.

"How were you pleased with us in the old synagogue?" asked Reb Schlome.

"It is a beautiful building, quiet and order prevails among you. I must express my thanks to you, I know I am only endebted to you for it, that I, a stranger student, was called upon to expound, an honour that this Saturday was only conceded to distinguished persons.... I obtained the names of all who were called upon to expound, they were universally men of weight and character, but with regard to the last, who was called upon just before me, no one would or could give me precise information, though all seemed to know him."

"I will explain that to you," said Schlome; "that man is a member of the well-known family of Nadler, a family that, even now I scarcely dare to say so, fifty years ago in spite of their wealth and prosperity was shunned by everyone. People would not associate with them. No one would marry their daughters, no one would converse with them, every one kept away from them in the houses of prayer; they could obtain no tenants; the very poor despised the alms which they would have lavished in abundant measure. You can easily divine the cause,--there rested on the grandfather of this unhappy family the weight of a suspicion which afterwards proved to be groundless, that he was one of those who cannot be received in the congregation of the Lord. The family suffered fearfully under this foregone conclusion. It was that great thinker, the high Rabbi Löw, who first devised a means of once for all dispelling the clouds of obloquy, in that he--it is this very Saturday exactly six-and-thirty years ago--in a lecture, with the approval of the ten chief personages of the then community, uttered a solemn curse against all those who should dare any longer to injure the reputation of the family, to speak evil of the dead, or to apply the name of Nadler as a contumelious epithet to any one in the Jewish community. From that day no one ventured to withdraw himself from intercourse with them, and all the more honour was shown to them that they consumed their wealth for the benefit of the poor and afflicted, lived strictly in accordance with the Law, and moreover people wished to make them forget the humiliation and injustice of many a long year. On this account people do not like to talk about them, and avoid everything that might lead to further explanations about this family."

Gabriel had listened in silence with the deepest sympathy. "See, Schöndel," Reb Schlome suddenly exclaimed, "I notice a very remarkable resemblance between Reb Gabriel and you, a resemblance, about which I yesterday by lamplight thought that I had been deceiving myself. In the middle of his forehead too a fiery spot is wont at times to gather."

"That is strange," said Gabriel earnestly and thoughtfully.

"Not so strange as you believe," struck in one of the guests, "it is a not uncommon appearance I have heard of one of the Imperialist officers who has a mark on his forehead, I think two crossed swords--probably your mother, when she carried you under her heart, saw a sudden conflagration, or is it an inherited family-mark; had your father also such a mark on his forehead?"

Gabriel had listened to the guest attentively, he gave no answer, but the red stripe of flame on his forehead became more conspicuous and clearly marked than before. "I myself," said the other guest by way of confirmation, "some years ago when I studied at the school in Mainz, knew a madman, named Jacob, and in his case too as soon as he became excited just such another mark made its appearance in the centre of his forehead; probably the concurring circumstances were the same with each of you."

"Moreover," added the guest, after a short consideration, "I fancy that I have seen that same madman in this very place."

"You are not mistaken," said Schöndel, "the mad Jacob is here in Prague, and our lodger Reb Gabriel can if he likes give us some news about him, for he has taken a great fancy to him, and often passes whole days with him without coming home or visiting the lecture-rooms."

It seemed for an instant as if Gabriel would have contradicted the goodwife, but he quickly recovered his self-possession and remained silent--at that moment the old maid-servant entered and announced a boy who was enquiring after Herr Gabriel Mar, and was urgently desirous of speaking to him.

"Excuse me," he said, rising quickly, "I must let the boy come to my room and hear what he has to say."

The boy must in fact have brought some important news, for Reb Gabriel did not return to table and sent his excuses by the old maid-servant-

-a soldier has arrived here from his country, such was the old Hannah's story, and he is breathlessly hurrying to hear, how it fares with all at home--the good student.

The two guests did not seem to share the old maid's favourable opinion. "A strange student that," opined one of them, "sits at table and speaks no word of his Talmudic investigations, gets up and does not pray, goes away and kisses no scroll."

Reb Schlome felt that his wife was right the other evening when she said, that Gabriel was less devout than other students, but he allowed this with reluctance, for Gabriel's rich stores of Talmudic science had won his estimation and good will. He requested, therefore, one of the two students to let them have a Talmudic discourse, and after this had been complied with recited the prayer after meat.

Gabriel had scarcely waited till the door of his room was shut to speak with the boy alone.

"What do you bring me, John," he asked hastily.

"Gracious Sir," answered the boy, "my relative begs respectfully to announce, that Ensign Herr Smil von Michalowitz is just arrived from Pilsen with a message to your Honour, and waits in your house."

"Good boy, run on, I will follow immediately."--Gabriel hastily donned cloak and cap and went out--Although the house which he was leaving was situated by the Old-synagogue and, therefore, outside of the Ghetto-gate, he was obliged to pass through the Ghetto in order to reach the Plattnergasse by the nearest route. He stopped at the back of a house. He knocked twice at a closed door; this was quickly opened, and he hurried up a back-staircase to a room, on the walls of which, sabres, travelling-pistols and other arms were hanging, crossed in varied confusion one upon the other. He threw off cloak and cap, girded a dagger about his loins, without lingering over the choice enveloped himself in a knight's mantle and stepped through a door in the tapestry into a large adjoining room. Here he was already expected. A slightly made young man in the embroidered uniform of one of Mannsfield's cavalry-officers was pacing impatiently up and down.--

"Welcome to Prague, Herr von Michalowitz," said Gabriel in a friendly way, "do you bring me good news from Mannsfield?"

"I wish I brought better, your Grace," answered the officer with a bow. "First of all, however, I have the honour to deliver the autograph despatch of the General-Fieldmarshal, I partly know its contents and am commissioned to give your Grace all further necessary explanations."

Gabriel hastily unsealed the despatch and cast a glance over its contents. "Our troops have still no pay," he cried, stamping his foot angrily, while the fiery mark on his forehead kindled to a deep red--"still nothing? and they promised me everything, money, munitions, forage, reinforcements. It's enough to drive a man mad! You would scarcely believe, Herr von Michalowitz, what a difficult position I am in here! Nothing can be done with this Frederick.--The Bohemians could not have elected a worse king.--He listens to his preachers, goes out hunting, gives banquets and tournaments--of Emperor and League he takes no heed.--His Generals are in constant feud with one another and only agree when it is a question of putting a slight upon or deposing Thurn and Mannsfield.--These gentlemen let me sue for reinforcements and plans of operation, as if they were things that concerned my own private advantage, as if I was asking an alms for myself. Believe me, Frederick must succumb. Who does he oppose to these experienced skilful Generals? an Anhalt against a Tilly, an Hohenlohe against a Boucquoi. The Bohemians are brave soldiers, but they are badly led. I can speak openly to you, Sir Ensign, who have been the constant confidant of our plans.--There is only one conceivable way for Frederick to get the upper-hand--Anhalt and Hohenlohe must be dismissed, and Matthias Thurn take the command."

"It is indeed melancholy," answered the Ensign bitterly, "that all our most energetic and best-laid efforts are so badly supported at Prague. This Anhalt gives up one strong position after another, and if things go on so, it is to be feared that Archduke Maximilian will drive the Prince in under the walls of Prague, and force him to accept a battle,--unless he has been entirely won over by the Imperialists--and a battle lost before the gates of Prague...."

"Would still not be decisive," interposed Gabriel. "I am well acquainted with Prague, it is strongly situated, and could hold out a long time.--I suppose you know the capital city of your native country? The citizens are brave, well-trained in arms, and in the old and new quarter at least devoted to the king's party.--Frederick's power is still great, Mannsfield manœuvres in the enemy's rear; fresh troops are on the march from Hungary.... Sir Ensign, say to my friend Mannsfield, that a battle lost before the gates of Prague would not put an end to the war;--but that Anhalt must not remain at the head of the army. So long as he commands in-chief, everything is at stake ... and to think that two such losers-of-armies as Anhalt and Hohenlohe should command thirty thousand men, while the hero Mannsfield, alone, forsaken by the Union and the weak Frederick for whom he is fighting, without support, without money, in an unknown country, surrounded by secret and open enemies, makes head with a small force against one three times his superior.--How does he bear the hard blows of fickle fortune?"

"With his usual calm, with unshakeable equanimity. Oh, there is but one Mannsfield, Sir Major-General, in such a hero alone do martial fame, and martial deeds attain so high a point. It is an event unparalleled in the annals of history, that a Count, first legitimized by the Emperor Rudolph, should defy the Emperor and whole Empire--should defy, without money, land, or support, under a ban, solitary, by the force of his sword and name alone.--What are all of us in Mannsfield's camp? are we the troops of the Union, which concluded on the 3d of July an ignominious peace with the league? are we the mercenaries of this Count Palatine, who placed the crown of our Fatherland upon his head for a merry pastime? By God and my knightly honour, no! What are we? we are nothing but Mannsfield's children, all of us, from the meanest artillery-driver up to you. Sir Major-General! We all cleave to him with faith as firm as a rock, we follow his standard alone, his call alone. We offer our lives for Mannsfield, his is our sword, our blood, our honour, our name, our oath; for well we know that he leads us on to naught but victory or an honourable soldier's death."

"You are very right. Sir Ensign," replied the General much moved, "he is to all of us a father, brother, friend! What should I have been if I had not fallen in with Mannsfield? Sir Ensign, you have a country, you have a coat of arms, you have a name--I had none of all this, I had nothing but my arm, and a revengeful, torn and bleeding heart!"--

"Yes, Sir Major-General, Mannsfield loves the bold, and brave, and among them are you numbered, by God, you have given good proof of that a thousand times! Name, rank and belief are indifferent to him; Mannsfield asks no questions whether a man is a Reformer, Utraquist or Lutheran, whether gentleman or knight, burgher or peasant, German or Bohemian? Consider, your Grace, that too forces me to admire Mannsfield.... has not this Frederick estranged the hearts of all Bohemians from him, in that he has by the advice of his sternly calvinistical intolerant Chaplain Abraham Schulz bitterly offended Catholics, Utraquists and Lutherans? I am a man of war and no scholar, I am a mere soldier, and have paid little attention to theology, but yet I hold that in this world, everyone should be allowed to believe what he likes, that is an affair to be settled by his own conscience; but no one should be permitted to be a hindrance and stumbling block to another, and throw ridicule upon that which is an object of respect and dear to his neighbour.... Why did we violently revolt from the illustrious House of Austria, under which we were great and powerful? Because we wished to be free to choose our faith, and now steps in this Frederick, whom we ourselves elected, whom we aggrandized, and we are no better off! Your Grace! You are no Bohemian and cannot comprehend, what a painful day the 3d of September in last year is to me, on which thirty-six lords, ninety-one knights and almost all the municipalities permitted themselves to be befooled by the brilliant eloquence of Wilhelm Raupowa and elected this incapable Frederick.--I too, as well as my uncle, the royal Burgrave, were among the voters."

The General was silent. Memories slumbered in his soul like sparks in a tinder; the lightest breath might kindle them to a clear blaze. The Ensign misinterpreted the silence. He had said much, that might have made an unpleasant impression upon the General. He was of low origin, no Bohemian, perhaps a co-religionist of the Palatine. "Your Grace," he therefore again began in an embarrassed way, after a short pause, "have I, perhaps, offended you? Are you, perchance, one of those, who busy themselves with religious studies, and learned ecclesiastical disputations? Are you, Sir Major-General, may I venture to ask, yourself a Calvinist? It's all the same to me, General, I should respect your high rank, your gallantry even if, you will excuse the joke, even if you were a Jew or a Heathen...."

Pictures out of a time that had long vanished again passed over Gabriel's soul, his spirit was again fast fixed on some moment of the distant past. "I busy myself no longer with religious studies," he answered, absently--"but at one time, at one time it was my highest enjoyment; but then I was still a J...." he did not finish, he seemed to awake suddenly from a heavy dream, a deep flush suffused his face, he stroked the hair off his high forehead, in the centre of which glowed the purple mark and added hastily in a changed voice: "then I was still young, very young--but now I think no more of it--and Mannsfield's faith is mine too."

The way in which the General spoke, the singular expression of his face, was not calculated to set at rest the Ensign's fears. "Your Grace!" he went on, "you yourself said in my presence that you had no name, when you took service in Mannsfield's corps, and yet now you are the Mannsfieldian General Otto Bitter, known and feared far and wide. It may be that, you have no genealogy, no past; but you have a future; with the point of your sword you inscribe your name on the brazen tablets of history."

"No, no," the General now impetuously continued, "no, not so. Herr von Michalowitz, believe me, I am not superstitious, not even a believer--I believe in actually nothing--do you hear! in actually nothing, but Mannsfield and mine own good sword.--I am not weak, I would not yield to any presentiment, but one presentiment does haunt me with all the strength of truth, as clear, as life-like as if I saw it with my own bodily eyes, *my name will not live in history*.... Mannsfield, Thurn, Boucquoi, Tilly, Waldstein, all the heroes that fight with us or against us, have lived for eternity, but my name will perish, will leave no trace behind it...."

The General paced the room many times and with his hand put back the dark locks from his high forehead, then stopped before the Ensign--"I sometimes become very excited, Herr von Michalowitz," he said, "and say much that would be better unsaid--therefore I pray you forget what I have spoken...."

The Ensign bowed in silence. The General threw himself into an arm-chair, motioned the Ensign also to a seat, and after a short pause took up Mannsfield's letter again. "You have captured another wandering Jew? You thought he was a spy, or messenger of the Imperialists, he carried letters in cipher with him?" asked the General, interrupting his reading.

"Yes, your Grace, the prisoner declares, improbably enough, the writings were Hebrew extracts from the Bible and letters to his wife.--The Field-Marshal sends the writings to you probably in the intention that you may prove their contents here in Prague with the assistance of some Rabbi, or clergyman learned in the Scripture." The Ensign with these words laid a sealed packet on the table. "We should almost prefer that he was guilty, in Pilsen, which is imperialist in feeling, we are quite surrounded by spies, we cannot any longer tell who to trust: an example of severity must be made."

The General involuntarily seized the packet, to unseal it, but quickly laid it aside, as if remembering himself, and read on.

"Sir Ensign, I must up to the castle," he said, when he had finished and maturely considered the despatch. "Nothing can be done with Anhalt and Hohenlohe--I must up, and once more speak with the king himself--To-morrow early you shall have the answer for Mannsfield."

"If your Grace will permit me I will accompany you to the castle."

The General rang the bell, a servant, who entered, was ordered to make the necessary preparation, and shortly afterwards the large principal entrance of the house, that led into the Marienplatz, was thrown open, and the General and Ensign rode out of it in the direction of the 'Kleinseite.' At a proper distance followed two mounted attendants armed with pistols and sabres.--

In King Frederick's anteroom three persons were waiting for an audience. They stood in the recess of a lofty bow-window, and were talking in a low voice but with much animation to one another.

"Yes, gentlemen," began John de Bubna, a man of some fifty years old, "yes, it is all Raupowa's fault. Your father--" he turned to the young Count Schlick--"the noble Count Joachim who voted for the Elector of Saxony was quite right--but the past is irreparable, and now we must defend ourselves to the last extremity. Our faith, our freedom, are at stake, is it not so, Thurn?"

The person thus addressed, Count Henry Mathias of Thurn was also of about the age of fifty. Dark eyes with all the fire of youth flashed from his bronzed countenance, as if to give the lie to the thick grey hair; the noble lineaments of his spiritual and thoughtful face showed at the first glance, that a hero's soul dwelt in this powerful and compact frame. He was indisputately the chief leader of his party, an able commander, and the originator of the revolt against the Emperor. It was he who brought about the well-known catastrophe of the 3d of May 1618, when the two Imperial stadtholders, Slawata and Martinitz, were thrown out of window into the court-yard, and supposing it is in the power of a single person, if not to evoke, at any rate to further a crisis on which the future history of the world may depend, Count Matthias Thurn was certainly one of those, who fanned the flames of this outbreak into that wild conflagration which devastated Germany and Central-Europe for thirty years.

He was by birth an Italian, but held rich possessions in Bohemia. A brave soldier, a practised courtier, a subtle diplomatist and excellent speaker, he had won the affections of the nobles, the army, and whole people, and the nation committed to him the weighty and influential place of a defender, or guardian of the faith. Deprived by the Emperor of his office, as Burgrave of Carlstein, he had later on assumed with Mannsfield the joint command of the Bohemian troops. Frederick, however, soon after his coronation, to the deep vexation of the Bohemian army, transferred the command to Prince Christian of Anhalt and Count George of Hohenlohe.

Count Thurn seemed to express his views unwillingly. "Yes, gentlemen, you know I was never the last in the field, I gladly combat for Bohemia. Perhaps a time will again come when I may fight for the cause--but in the meanwhile...."

"Your Grace then is absolutely determined not to accept a command so long as the Prince commands in-chief?" asked Henry Schlick hastily.

"He is right," opined John Bubna; "it was a stupid course of the king, to take the command from our Thurn."

"It is not that," continued Thurn, "at least not that alone; but the war is badly conducted. What did I and young Anhalt, who is far superior to his father in gallantry, and in spite of his youth in military science too, what did we insist upon in the council of war at Rokizan; that we should fall with our whole force upon an enemy wearied out with painful marching. Even Hohenlohe, who is usually very reluctant to embrace a bold project, shared our opinion--there could not be a doubt, we must have gained a victory--then up gets Prince Anhalt and proved to the king in a long speech--but, I cannot bear to think of it, how my splendid plan of operations was frustrated, how instead of fighting they allowed themselves to become involved in a disgraceful treaty, how we, I may say, fled to Unhoscht without striking a blow, or if it sounds better, drew back in good order; for the slight affair at Rakoniz, where, moreover, we lost von Dohna and Graz, cannot be counted anything."

"But the rencounter at Rakoniz," observed Henry Schlick, "remained, as I have heard, undecided. The Imperialists too lost both their Field-Marshals Fugger and Aguaviva; and their General-in-chief Boucquoi was so severely wounded as to have been since incapable of bearing a campaign."

"Sir Count," replied Thurn moodily, "you do not know Boucquoi, he is a worthy antagonist of the very bravest. If it comes to a battle, he will be carried though in a dying state to the field. God grant, that we may not shortly see him before the gates of Prague. At Unhoscht," resumed Thurn, "my patience was exhausted, and when the king, at Anhalt's urgent request went to Prague, I offered to accompany him. I am glad to be here and--"

Thurn was interrupted, for the door of the antechamber opened, and Gabriel, or Mannsfield's Major-General Otto Bitter entered.

"Ah, welcome friend," cried John Bubna, held out his hand to him and led him up to the two others. "Do not be put out, Count Thurn, I answer for my friend Bitter, go on with what you were saying."

"I am acquainted with the Major-General," said Thurn, while Bitter made a low obeisance.--"My friend's friend is my friend too."--Then Thurn himself with obliging civility presented the young men to one another, "Count Henry Schlick, son of our supreme Judge and Director, the Lord Joachim Andrew Schlick, Count of Passau and Ellbogen, a brave captain--Sir Otto Bitter, Major-General in Mannsfield's army and his right hand man."--

"The name of Schlick," said Otto Bitter politely, "has a genuine ring about it, and you, Sir Captain, as I have been assured on all sides, are worthy of bearing so celebrated a name."

Henry Schlick wished to respond to the General's courteous address, but Matthias Thurn turned to him and asked what brought him to Prague.

"I make no secret of my mission," he answered, "I am come to Prague under instructions from the Field-Marshal to demand the pay of our troops, which is now nearly six months in arrear, and to remind them of the promised reinforcements; I propose to stay here just long enough to urge upon the king and his generals some decisive step which our Mannsfield will support with all his might; but the king is too busy with his festivities, and Field-Marshal Prince Anhalt, has, at least for me, no time unoccupied."

"Hush!" said Bubna, "lupus in fabula, he comes just in...."

The conversation, though it had been carried on in an undertone, was instantly dropped. The double doors of the antechamber were thrown hastily and noisily open, and Prince Christian of Anhalt, Commander-in-chief of the royal army and Stadtholder of Prague, stepped haughtily with a proud look into the anteroom. All present, with the exception of Thurn made a low bow. Anhalt recognised it with a careless nod of the head, and prepared as usual to enter unannounced into the royal apartment. Otto Bitter, however, advanced hastily and said:

"I am fortunate in meeting your Highness here. I am just arrived from General-Field-Marshal the Count of Mannsfield...."

"You have come from Count Mannsfield?" repeated the Prince with a sharp emphasis. "Why does not he make his applications immediately to the commander-in-chief, as every commander of a corps d'armée should do. What is the use of a mediator and go-between? Besides, time and place are very badly chosen for your representations, this is the king's anteroom, and I am on my way to an audience"--so saying, Anhalt, without allowing the General time to reply, passed into the king's audience-chamber. Bitter returned to the other lords; his features were disfigured by rage, and the fiery sign burnt red upon his forehead. All were unpleasantly affected by this behaviour.

"Such is the manner of princes," Henry Schlick tried to make a conciliatory excuse; "he is imperious and hates opposition, do not be so put out by it, Sir Major-General."

"No! to receive an officer of such high desert in such a way," exclaimed Bubna clashing his scabbard upon the floor; "and when he was speaking of Mannsfield!..."

"These men of the Palatinate have always free access to the king," observed Thurn, and out of his eyes flashed, as it were, a consuming lightning--"and as for us, they let us wait."

Andrew of Habernfeld, Frederick's favorite, in full gala-costume, opened at the very moment the door of the king's apartment; he might probably have heard this last observation of Thurn's, spoken in a loud voice.

"Can audience be obtained of his Majesty," asked Thurn drawing himself up proudly, "I mean, by us...."

"The king cannot be aware, that so many gentlemen of the highest dignity wish to speak with him, or else he had surely before this summoned you before him. I will immediately inform him of your presence."

"Bubna, Schlick, and I, have been announced long since and been kept waiting in vain up to this time," replied Thurn stiffly, "Major-General Bitter is also apparently as desirous as we are of an interview with the king.--Meantime it can do no harm if you once more remind him of our presence."

Habernfeld looked very much disconcerted and instantly disappeared. Shortly afterwards he returned breathless. "His Majesty," he announced, "implores the noble lords to spare him all government-business at present. The king celebrates today the anniversary of his arrival in Prague, and invites the lords to betake themselves to the banquet in the hall of Spain."

"A banquet?" replied Thurn almost sadly, and the veins on his noble forehead swelled high; "I am sorry not to be able to accept the gracious invitation, I am not in a humour for banqueting, my thoughts would be ever occupied with the victorious irresistible advance of the Imperialists, and my gloomy face would but mar the festal joy, give this answer to the king, I pray you, do so, Herr von Habernfeld.... that he may graciously excuse my absence...." with these words Thurn threw his cloak over his shoulder, and would have departed.

"Your Grace," cried Schlick, seizing Thurn by the arm, "on every account, pause. He is our lord and king--our self-elected lord and king, he will take it in very bad part."

"My young friend," whispered Thurn in Schlick's ear--"spare me the hated sight of Anhalt carousing by the side of king, while our brave army is offering itself a vain sacrifice. Meat and drink would become poison and gall to me.--You know, I am not easily induced to change a determination that I have once made, therefore, I pray you, Sir Count, leave me."

"I will at least present your humble excuses to the king's Majesty," answered Schlick aloud; "I pray you, Herr von Habernfeld, forget, what the Count may have said in a moment of excitement, he is a warm patriot, a staunch Bohemian, but still the southern blood of Italy flows in his veins."

Thurn went away, the three gentlemen followed Habernfeld to the banqueting-hall. Twilight had in the meanwhile come on. The broad and spacious room was illuminated, fairy-like, with a thousand waxen torches. The rich sea of light broke into countless points of brilliancy upon the lofty mirrors. A sumptuous circle of ladies and gentlemen, mostly from the Palatinate and Germany, passed with merry laughter through the gorgeously ornamented apartment. No one seemed to think of the war--to judge from the attitude of those who were present no one could have had a presentiment that in eight days all this splendor would have disappeared.

At the upper end of the hall was a throne-like elevation, where King Frederick and his spouse sat on two crimson and gold-embroidered chairs of state. They were a wonderful pair. Frederick was then in his twenty-fifth year. Fair waving locks, mild blue eyes, and soft rosy cheeks, gave to his features, an air of weakness, almost effeminacy--and yet the carefully arranged blond mustachio and whiskers became him wonderfully. The costume of the period was especially adapted to set off the advantages of his person in the best light. He was entirely dressed in a suit of dark violet coloured velvet. The close fitting doublet was richly embroidered with gold, the slashed armlets lined with white were ornamented with point-lace. Over a white lace collar hung a gold medallion attached by a red ribbon. The trowsers, cut short at the knee, were there adorned with gold brocade and point-lace. In his left hand he held a black cap with red and white feathers.

Queen Elisabeth was somewhat smaller than Frederick. She was a perfect beauty. Her face bore the stamp of her English origin. Abundant fair golden hair, into which a diadem had been woven by a blue ribbon, cheeks suffused with the most delicate pink, lovely soft blue eyes, gave to the queen at first sight a remarkable resemblance to her husband. She wore a dress of pale green satin. This, low bodied and close fitting, brought out the wonderful fulness of her contour. The string of pearls, that hung round her neck, seemed to flow without any perceptible division into the snowy whiteness of her bosom.--Both, Frederick and his consort, wore satin shoes with large silk bows, and their feet rested upon a crimson cushion.--They gazed cheerfully and good-naturedly at the varied throng. Musicians occupied the gallery and at a sign from Habernfeld, on the entrance of the three officers, struck up a clamorous flourish of trumpets, and then played lively tunes.

The three officers in their simple uniform made a striking contrast to the rest of the company. Henry Schlick as fine a courtier, as a brave soldier, soon made himself at home among a group of ladies, but Bubna and Bitter felt strange amid the loud hubbub of the assembled guests, and stared silently and gloomily straight before them. Immediately on their arrival Habernfeld had led all three of them up to the place where the king was sitting and Schlick had excused the absence of Count Thurn on the score of urgent business that could not be postponed. General Bitter dared not venture on this occasion to announce the aim of his mission to Prague, but was fully determined in the course of the evening to submit his business to the king. An opportunity soon offered. The king and queen rose from their seats in order to make a tour of the room, and those who were present--for Frederick popular and condescending was fond of saying a word to each--ranged themselves in two long rows. The king, whom the Prince of Anhalt followed at a short distance, began to move down the line of gentlemen, while the queen turned to that of the ladies. Everyone to whom the king addressed an observation made a low obeisance. He spoke to everybody, and had a friendly or flattering word for each. Bitter and Bubna had remained standing together and waited in respectful silence for Frederick's address. As he approached General Bitter, Anhalt whispered something in the king's ear.

"General Bitter, from Mannsfield's camp, is it not so?" asked Frederick, while a shade of vexation flitted over his face--"I am pleased to see you in Prague; but you have been some weeks here. I am surprised that they can do so long without you in Mannsfield's camp...."

Bubna bit his lips till the blood started; and Bitter answered undismayed but calmly:

"Since your royal Majesty is so gracious as to enquire the grounds of my long residence in Prague, I must most humbly take leave to mention the affairs, that I have already once before had the honour of most obediently laying before your royal Majesty...."

"No business, no business," said Frederick, so loud that the bystanders could hear it, "I will for once in my life be joyous and not always thinking of governing and commanding. For the rest," he continued with excitement, "complaints are abroad; that Mannsfield places the district round about Pilsen under contribution as if he were in an enemy's country, and oppresses my own people: a stop must be put to this."

"If your Majesty will only listen to me for a moment," said Bitter hastily. "Mannsfield's corps d'armée is made up mainly of foreigners; bound by no oath to the crown of Bohemia they fight only so long as they receive pay. The pay is six months in arrear, the famished soldier, who has not a whole coat to his body, resembles rather a ragged robber than a man-at-arms, and if Mannsfield were not the adored hero of our camp, the whole corps would long ago have freed itself from the bands of discipline.--We are also surrounded by enemies, for Pilsen and the circumjacent districts are Imperialist in their sympathies, and the storming of Pilsen cost us many a bloody battle and many a skirmish.--The peasants, who should deliver corn and forage, and have up to this time been vainly paid by assignments upon the money that was to come from Prague, are difficult to deal with, and stand up in arms against us in large masses. All the necessaries of life have to be violently procured, sword in hand, out of a hostile and almost exhausted circle.--Your Majesty in your high wisdom cannot really expect that Mannsfield could obtain food for four thousand men and one thousand five hundred horses empty handed. As soon as your Majesty shall have graciously condescended to give orders to your commander-in-chief and paymaster, to pay over to us the sum that is due, there will be an end of all violence, and compensation will be made to those who have been aggrieved. To lay this and one other petition before your royal Majesty am I come to Prague, and as I have not yet been so fortunate as to see the object of my visit crowned with success, I was to my sorrow obliged to determine to remain absent for a time from the army, though every officer, every commander, should stay with his troops."

Anhalt grew pale with anger. Frederick was silent for a moment; the frank unconstrained speech of Mannsfield's officer had surprised and for a moment disturbed his composure.

"You speak very openly and unconstrainedly, Sir General,--I love frankness in a soldier, but you should never transgress the bounds of due respect. I will talk over and consider what you have said to me with my commander-in-chief.--When you return to Mannsfield's camp, do not report to the troops the manner in which you have addressed me--it might injure respect."

Frederick pronounced these words with a sad smile in an undertone, almost in a whisper inaudible to the rest.--He went no farther down the line, the joy of the evening was troubled, the king and queen soon went away, and Bubna and Bitter were the first to follow their example.

"Pest upon the Palatine," cried Bubna furiously, as both together rode down the Spornergasse. "But you stood up stoutly, Bitter: answered word for word and bravely urged your suit. That Frederick stood before thee trembling like a school-boy! *He* talk of oppression and forced contributions, and leaves his own brave troops to perish of hunger!--I cannot find fault with Thurn for having broken quite loose from this luxurious court, and shall wait till he returns again to the helm.--God be merciful to our poor country!"

Before Bubna's house the two Generals took leave of one another, and Bitter alone, followed by his two mounted servants, galloped over the bridge to the Altstadt. As he arrived at the Marienplatz, the clapper of the clock in the tower struck twenty one, equivalent to nine o'clock in the evening.--The owner of the house was waiting for him at the great gate, an armourer, who in times past had served under him as sergeant-major.

"It is already late," whispered Bitter to him, as he rode in, "open the back-door directly, I must be quick."--Shortly thereupon Otto Bitter stepped out of the back-door that led into the Plattnergasse; he wore again the dress of a student and hurried quickly to the Jews-quarter. The proprietor of the house, a man with a wooden leg, closed the door carefully and grumbled as he went across the court: "My general is brave, second to none as a warrior, but this passion is rather despicable for a great lord, now if it were a count's daughter or a lady of rank: but a Jewish wench! I cannot understand it."

Gabriel struck into the shortest way to his dwelling by the Old-Synagogue, he found the gate of the Ghetto still open and passed through the gate in the street called "golden" into it.--He had walked a short distance sunk in deep thought, when suddenly some words struck his ear: "I thank you, dear lady, I cannot accept your company, it is here, I think, quite safe in the streets and I shall soon be at home."

The melodious ringing tone of this voice made an extraordinary impression upon Gabriel. A violent terror for a moment thrilled through him. The strong colossal man was obliged to lean against a wall in order to save himself from falling, his breast heaved with mighty respirations, it seemed as if he did not dare to look about him, as if he was afraid that the form to which that voice belonged would melt before his eyes into nothing. But at the next moment a woman passed quickly by him, and the moon, gliding at that moment from behind a cloud, threw its pale trembling light upon a face that was, as it chanced, but half concealed by a floating veil. He could recognise the features, his ear had not deceived him.--"Found," he cried almost aloud after a pause of speechless rapture; "Gabriel! thou hast drained the cup of sorrow to the dregs! But thy revenge will be sweet, will be fearful!" ... then he followed, unobserved, with hasty step, the woman's form. She stopped for the first time breathless at the Hahnpass before an apparently quite uninhabited dilapidated three-storied house. She opened the house-door with a key that she drew out of a pocket in her dress, and shortly afterwards Gabriel saw a ray of light shooting from a garret-window. Gabriel wiped the perspiration from his forehead, rubbed his eyes, looked about him, laid his hands upon the cold walls of the house in order to convince himself that it was no dream, that filled him with lying phantoms, that this moment had really and truly an actual existence. He might have stood there for some few minutes when again the clear accents of a woman's voice pierced his ear.--"Why do you stand dreaming there, Reb Gabriel?"

Gabriel awoke as from a heavy sleep; a group of women stood before him, among them, his hostess Schöndel. "Why do you stand in the street like this, what are you waiting for? Why have you been neither home nor to service in the Old-Synagogue since mid-day?"

Gabriel recovered himself quickly; he found himself in the neighbourhood of Jacob's house; he had frequently excused his staying away so long from Schlome's house on the plea of his visits to the lunatic; he, unsociable as he was, never conversed with anyone, and Gabriel could feel sure that he would not be betrayed by him at any rate.

"Cannot you see," he said, "I have just come from the poor lunatic, who enlists my sympathies in the highest degree. One should visit those who are afflicted with spiritual infirmities, as well as those who suffer bodily ailment, and, perhaps, to do so is a more excellent work of charity."

"We too return from doing a good action," replied Schöndel; "I belong to the society of 'devout women.' We have been praying at the death-bed of a departing sister, have closed the eyes of a poor forsaken old woman.--It is sad to die solitary and forsaken."--Schöndel dried her beautiful eyes, which were wet with emotion.

"We must make haste," said a woman, a neighbour of Schöndels', "or the gate will be shut, we are the only people who live outside...."

"Reb Gabriel, if you are going home too, give us your company," said Schöndel.

Gabriel walked silently and rapt in meditation by the side of the two women, while they, full of the recollection of the sad duty which they had just performed, did not attempt to resume the conversation.

Arrived at home Schöndel told her husband, how she had found Gabriel at the door of the lunatic's house, with whom he had spent the afternoon and evening.--Gabriel threw himself, as soon as he reached his room, in a more than feverish state of excitement into a chair. The manifold events of the day all disappeared before the extraordinary impression that the discovery of that woman had made upon him.--He staid awake the whole night, pacing the room backwards and forwards and only towards morning could make up his mind to write the report which Ensign Michalowitz was to carry back to Count Mannsfield.

Chapter IV

In the garret of a usually uninhabited dilapidated three-storied house in the Hahnpass a woman was sitting at a rickety table and embroidering by the light of an oil-lamp a curtain for the holy tabernacle. It was already late; a rude wind howled through the walls of the poor dwelling, a corner house, far over-topping all the others. All was dark in the vicinity, only the windows of the distant lecture-room which was visited by a succession of students emitted a dull light. The woman, though no longer in the first bloom of youth, presented a perfect picture of the most faultless oriental beauty. She might have numbered six or eight and twenty years. Her wonderfully well-formed face, pale as a lily, but suffused from time to time with the softest roseate flush, contrasted superbly with the shining black hair, the rich waving curls of which issued from under a turban-like head-dress and fell in waves on her snowy neck. Her eyes were brighter and blacker than coal, her eyelids fringed with long silky lashes, and her half-opened fresh lips disclosed two rows of pearly teeth.--She worked assiduously, only interrupting herself now and then to go to the open door of a second chamber and listen to the breathing of her sleeping mother--or when she lent with an expression of the deepest motherly love over a cradle, in which a baby, the perfect image of its mother was sleeping quietly.

"Blume, my child," now cried the mother from the adjacent room, "are you still up? Go to bed, spare your eyes, I pray you do so.--When a person has lived as I have done for more than fifteen years in darkness, she learns for the first time to set a right value on eyesight, take my advice, child, go to bed!"

"Only go thou to sleep, dear mother," answered Blume in a loud voice, almost screaming, and leaving off her work for a few moments. "It is not so late as you think, it wants two hours yet to midnight."

"If only your husband would return from his journey," sighed the mother, "he would surely bring money with him, and you would no longer consider it necessary to make a sacrifice of your sweet precious sight.--Lord of the world! that a Rottenberg should be reduced to travel over the country as a scribe in order to earn a livelihood, that my daughter, my graceful Blume, must work at embroidery to save herself from beggary, that grieves me--but Lord, Thou art just, and what Thou doest, is well done, I do not murmur! I only make my supplication before Thee out of the profoundest depths of my heart, not for myself, not for myself, who am tottering on the verge of the grave, but for my children--have mercy upon them!"

"Sleep, dear mother, sleep," cried Blume, and large tears fell like pearls over her cheeks, "all will come right, believe me, God never forsakes his own."

Blume shut the door. "Yes, if only my husband were at home again," said she then, with a shiver; "sometimes I become so sad when I am alone with my mother and child, alone, forsaken, in a strange and unknown city! and my husband wanders over the country to earn bread; God preserve him."

She folded her hands almost involuntarily and began the evening prayer with fervent devotion. The little slumberer in the cradle awoke and cried after its mother. Without interrupting her prayer she suckled it.--She was just saying the words, "May the Everlasting bless and guard thee! May he let the light of His countenance shine upon thee and be gracious unto thee, may the Everlasting turn His face to thee and give thee peace for evermore," as she pressed the child to her bosom, and falling tears bedewed the babe's lovely face.--Suddenly it seemed to her as if the house-door was opened--could it be her husband returned from his journey? that was inconceivable--a man's step sounded upon the contiguous staircase, she heard a noise, as if some one was groping for the latch and could not find it.... Who could be seeking the stranger and friendless woman? a nameless pang for a moment seized her heart,--she was at the conclusion of the evening prayer, and the last words of the same filled her again with the confidence of faith, she said them, perhaps unconsciously, aloud, "Into thy hands I commend my spirit, sleeping or waking, my soul and body.... God is with me, therefore, I cannot fear!" She kept her eyes fixed fast upon the entrance. As a weak wooden bolt fastened the door on the inside, she expected, that the comer would first knock; but it happened otherwise, and a single push from a strong hand made the door come open.

"Gabriel," cried Blume, the colour forsaking her lips, with a suppressed cry of the most hopeless despair; she tore the child from her breast, which she hurriedly covered, pressed it tight in her arms, and got up as though she feared that Gabriel would tear it away from her.

He stood speechless and as one rooted to the ground before her--his whole body trembled, a strange and wonderful quivering passed over his pale corpse-like face, his eyes flashed lightning, the fiery mark on his forehead glowed, his broad breast rose and sank stormily, an unchained passion seemed to rage within him--for some moments he vainly strove to speak.

"I am he," he said at length in a hollow voice, and each word sounded in the ear of the terrified woman like the roar of thunder; "I am Gabriel Süss--whom ye all expelled and trampled upon.--Thou too.--Thou! whom I had once so deeply and ardently loved."

A long pause again ensued, Blume's bosom heaved impetuously, she stared at Gabriel, as if he were some horrible spectre; she held her child still tightly pressed to her; at length she broke the painful silence and spoke in a soft imploring voice: "That is past and gone, Gabriel.... What do you want of me now?"

"Thee!"

The poor tortured woman sank upon her chair. Gabriel paced the chamber several times.

"Do not waken my blind mother, Gabriel," prayed Blume, at length timidly and in a voice scarce audible; "age and sickness have weakened her sense of hearing, but you speak so loudly, so impetuously...."

"Shut the door closer, I must speak with thee alone, no third person shall hear us...."

Blume shut the door. "Gabriel," she said with trembling voice, "I am alone with you, I am a weak woman, you are a giant in strength--but never forget--a third person does hear us, does see us--the spirit of the Lord is over all--he is near to them which are afflicted, he helps the oppressed."

Gabriel did not interrupt her; but an incredulous smile so horribly disfigured his once beautiful features, the fiery mark on his forehead blazed out so strangely from under his dark hair that the word died away on her lips..... she felt that an hatred nourished for years in all its force held irresistible dominion in Gabriel's breast, and that he was now vainly striving to find an expression for that wild consuming ardour of vengeance that drove his hot blood to the height of madness! The baby had again dropped fast asleep, Blume did not know what to do, she dared not lay the child in its cradle.

"Is that.... thy only child?" Gabriel recommenced after a profound silence with that singular inexplicable aberration of thoughts which sometimes seems to come over a man at the very moment when the overpowering sensations of the moment should in fullest measure occupy his mental activity.

"It is my only dear innocent child," cried Blume in mortal terror and bursting into tears--"let me take it to my mother that we may not awake it."--

"Blume!" shouted Gabriel, seizing her arm and detaining her, "there are two words that I will never hear from your mouth 'mother' and 'innocent child', do not utter them in my presence, or you may make me forget resolves that have been ripening for years, and take once for all a fearful vengeance on thee and thy child.... 'Mother'" repeated Gabriel in a voice so sad and piercing that even Blume pitied him, "'mother' that beautiful sweet heavenly word, which everyone utters and hears so gladly--that word, which finds its way into the depths of the heart, and evokes in everyone an inexpressible feeling of bliss. 'Mother' that word, which ringing through the spheres awakes a magic harmony in the soul--that word is to me an empty hollow meaningless sound! Every man, as far as the blue vault of heaven overarches the earth, even though he were the wretchedest slave, that shakes his chain in maniacal fury, every living being, all, all, all have or have had a mother----only I not! only I not, I alone since men have walked the earth! The woman, the abandoned creature, the demon.... that thrust me into this existence.... she was no mother! Fye, fye, call her not mother! apply not the beautiful glorious name to her!--a mother--though it were the spotted hyena that destroys in mere wantonness, a mother defends her offspring.... a mother does not pile the whole weight of the sins which she has committed upon her child's innocent head, while it stands wringing its hands, in despair at her deathbed--a mother...."

"Gabriel, hush! for God's sake, say no more.... speak no more so of thy mother, my mother's sister. In spite of all she is thy mother, thou art her son! she is dead, be not hard upon her--a day will come, when thou too wilt stand before the judgment seat of the most High, when thou too wilt implore the mercy, the grace of God. Oh, think of that! The moments of each mortal existence are numbered.... think on the last hours of thy life!... hadst thou in thy storm-tossed life never sinned, hadst thou never committed a fault, never--save to speak thus of thy mother, of thy mother that carried thee in her womb, bore thee in pain, nourished, nursed, loved.... hadst thou committed no fault but in speaking thus of thy mother.... Gabriel, thou must tremble at the thought of the world to come."

Blume spoke these words with noble indignation, with the impulsive enthusiasm of a prophetess, her cheeks glowed, her eyes sparkled, she resembled a supernatural being.

"Woman!" replied Gabriel, with flashing glance, "I do not tremble!... I have looked death in the face thousands of times in the whirl of battle and did not tremble, thousands have fallen beside me mutilated by the enemies' cannon, their scattered brains have sprinkled my face, and I did not tremble--I was surrounded by bands of foes, all pointed their swords at my breast, I was wounded, seemed lost--I slew them all but did not tremble."

"But you are alive, it was not your last moment," interposed Blume hastily,--"but by the Almighty God of Israel, who made the worlds above, and will hereafter awaken those who slumber below," she pointed up to the blue dome of heaven, down to the graves of the snow-covered burial-ground seen from her window--"by his holy name--*when thy last hour strikes, in the last moment of thy life thou wilt tremble, repentance will break thy proud unbending heart*."

Gabriel was silent, "let us quit the vain contention of priests, of Rabbis," he said at length, involuntarily in a milder tone: "Thou hast never troubled thyself about my life--leave to me the care of my hour of death--what signifies it to thee? Wilt thou be near me in my last hour? wilt thou close my wearied eyes? wilt thou scare the ravens from my bloody corpse, when I lie on the field of battle trampled under the hoofs of horses? What carest thou for me and my soul's salvation? What carest thou for the stranger, the outcast? Long, long is it vanished, the beautiful golden time when it would have been otherwise...."

Gabriel spoke again with measureless impetuosity, but yet in his last words a deeply agitated expression of sorrow had wonderfully mingled itself with the wild rage, and even Blume, the noble loyal wife, was much touched, she perceived how this stony man had once loved her, how fruitful in misery his past life must have been!

"You are alone? Your husband is absent? Do you know where he is?" asked Gabriel after a pause, apparently calm.

Blume was convulsed again with a fearful terror and answered humbly: "He travels about as a scribe to earn us bread. I do not know where he is, I have no news of him--have compassion upon us, Gabriel, the Rottenbergs are no longer rich, we are poor and wretched."

Gabriel gazed awhile darkly before him, then suddenly, as if embracing a violent resolution, stood before Blume and pressed her down on a chair.

"Woman," he said, "for ten years have I sought thee, ten years have I panted to see thee, to speak with thee, to be avenged on thee, as the wounded, exhausted hart for fresh water.--When I saw at a distance the towers of Prague, where I knew that I should find thee, when I entered the Ghetto whose gates enclosed thee--then my heart bounded with a wild joy, I assumed the dress of a student, I visited all the houses of prayer, the lecture-rooms, the libraries, in order to meet your husband. I dwelt with those to whom I bear a deadly hate, all this only--to find thee.... I despised not to associate with a mad beggar, because I believed he would put me upon your track--when I recognised you yesterday evening, I was so happy in my hate, so superabundantly happy, to have found thee, to have revenge in my power--happy! as I have never been since that fateful hour when all the hope of my life was quenched and now, now that I stand before thee, that my hands clasp thy beautiful rounded arm, now, at this moment words fail me to tell thee, how fervently I hate thee, how fervently I hate ye all...."

Gabriel again paced up and down in the highest excitement. "I will tell you a story, Blume," he said at length, pushing a chair by her side, "a very notable story, most of it you already know, but it matters not, it is long since the history has crossed my lips, and I will once more bring my comfortless past before my soul, perchance in so doing I shall find the true expression for that emotion which agitates my breast.--Once upon a time there lived in Cologne a man named Baruch Süss. He was physician to the Archbishop, rich, powerful, and respected at court. But he was prouder of the possession of two daughters, Miriam and Perl, than of his wealth and influence. On the death of two hopeful boys he had transferred to them his whole love. They were the most beauteous maidens in Germany, and suitors soon approached them from all corners of the world. Miriam could with difficulty make up her mind, and only after the younger, Perl, your mother, had intermarried with a branch of the celebrated Rottenberg family, did her father succeed in fixing her choice upon his brother's son, his nephew, Joseph Süss, who lived at Spires.--Their marriage was for three years a childless one, in the fourth she announced to her enraptured husband that she was a mother.--Miriam Süss was brought to bed of a wonderfully beautiful boy, they named him Gabriel. The happy husband rejoiced, the poor were bountifully endowed, a rich foundation established. Baruch of Cologne, the grandfather, who before had feared that he would remain without posterity, undertook the fatiguing journey to Spires for the express purpose of seeing his first grandchild, and in the first intoxication settled his property upon him after his death. Shortly after me, you, Blume, were born, and the grandfather and his two sons-in-law agreed, that the children should some day be united in the bond of wedlock. The years of my childhood and of my youth flew happily by. Idolised by a father whose rich love I could not, though with the best intentions, adequately return, I clave with an infelt warm and holy love to my mother, who guarded me as the apple of her eye. Both because I remained an only child, and on account of my intended union with you, Blume, who wast also the only child of thy parents, my grandfather heaped all his tenderness upon my head. I remember but dimly my earliest childhood, and only one circumstance presents itself to my soul, but so mistily, so confusedly, that even to this day I am in doubt, whether it was not a dream, a deceitful phantom, that my glowing fancy at a later period created and then referred back to an earlier time. I was once walking outside the gate, accompanied as usual by a maidservant, when suddenly a tall, pale, thin man threw himself upon me, pressed me to his heart, and dropped two large tears upon my face. My nursemaid, as surprised as I, would have screamed, but he pressed a piece of gold into her hand and speedily made off with a heavy sigh.--If it was not a dream, that man was my father!"

Gabriel stopped exhausted. Blume was acquainted with her kinsman's early history, she followed his narrative with the most strained attention, anxiously awaiting the moment when he should come to the most fearful catastrophe of his life.

"You know," continued Gabriel, "that from my ninth year I passed one half of the year with my grandfather, the other in my parents' house. My education was a perfect one. In Spires I was thoroughly instructed in religious and Talmudic knowledge; my grandfather, loved and respected at the Court of the Archbishop of Cologne, and owing to his situation, for a Jew a peculiar one, in constant intercourse with the Rhenish nobility, caused me to be indoctrinated with all those sciences, that are ordinarily less accessible to German Jews. I even dared devote myself to knightly arts and exercises, forbidden them in the largest portion of Germany either by law or arbitrarily. I was well made, strong, gifted with a keen and penetrating spirit. I was nineteen years old, and once, it was on the feast of the dedication, on my return home from the high-school at Frankfurt, I found my grandfather there. It had with wise foresight--not to arouse my opposition before hand--been kept secret from me that they intended to marry me to you whom I had never seen before, and even then when it was announced that we were all to go and visit uncle Joel in Worms, it never in the least occurred to me, that the journey was to be a bridal one for me. We arrived at Worms. I saw you, Blume! resplendent with all the lustre of your youthful beauty, and the deepest love that ever seized man's heart blazed suddenly high in my bosom. To my mother's husband who called himself my father I had only devoted a feeling of gratitude, not of inclination, and it was my, your grandfather, to whom I openly declared my ardent affection, and that I believed it to be returned. 'My glorious, my dear child,' exclaimed the old man and tears streamed from his eyes, 'by thee all the wishes of my heart are fulfilled; yes, Gabriel! Blume, thy mother's sister's daughter, is the bride that was destined for thee. God bless the union, that your fathers concluded upon in your earliest years, and that you have sealed by the feelings of your heart.' Holding my grandfather's hand I stood before you, and dared to kiss your forehead white as alabaster. We were bride and bridegroom...."

Gabriel made another pause. Blume's face revealed the fearful anguish of her soul, she knew, what would follow, and cold clear drops of perspiration trickled down her face, which even the bitterest mental torture could not rob of its miraculous attractiveness. Her heart beat audibly.

"I was the happiest man on earth," continued Gabriel in a voice, the unsteadiness of which was a sign of the infinite sorrow that consumed his soul, "I was filled with my faith to which I clave with all the strength of my mind and spirit. It made me happy, it exalted me. I had a mother, and I loved my mother with that unutterable superhuman intenseness, for which we vainly seek an expression, which can only exist to such a pitch in the heart of a grateful child. I had thee, and how I loved thee, how I loved thee, Blume! That thou hast never had an idea of, that thou couldst never have had an idea of!..."

Gabriel stopped short, his voice, that in the whirl of battle could be heard above the thunder of the cannon, sounded feeble and tremulous; his gleaming eyes were wet. He passed his hand over his forehead, and went on: "It was doomed to be otherwise. Ten months had elapsed since our betrothal, I was at Worms, on a visit to you, and full of hope was looking towards a future close at hand, in which you were to be wedded to me; when an unexpected message arrived, that my mother had been suddenly attacked by a mortal sickness, that I was to make haste, if I would see her again alive. A maddening grief thrilled through my breast. I flew along the road to Spires, like one hunted by evil shadows; I arrived late on the evening of the new year. The servants were waiting for me in the entrance-hall, they wished to delay me, to prepare me; I paid no heed to their officiousness, and flew breathless and swift as an arrow up the stairs and into my mother's sick-room. She was still living, but lay at her last gasp. The darkness was broken: many men had already assembled to say the prayers for a departing soul,--the chamber was lit by a pendant lamp of eight branches in the centre of it. Joseph Süss stood by her bed and held her hands in his. The sorrowful consolation of finding her still alive struggled in me with the bitterest grief 'Here am I, dear Mother,' I cried in a voice choked by tears, throwing myself on my knees before her, and covering her beautiful cold hand with hot kisses, 'here am I, good sweet mother! I was sure that thou wouldst tarry for thine own true son.... I could not believe, dear true-hearted mother, that thou wouldest soar away from me before I arrived.... here I am, here I kneel before thee in deep inexpressible sorrow. Why do you not speak to me?... Look at me once again, only once again, with thy mild loved eye, speak to me I implore you! only one word, but one, a last farewell ... lay thine hand in blessing on the head of thy only child, whom thou forsakest, who is dying of deep and infinite grief!..."

"The bye-standers, though accustomed to scenes of death, were constrained to sob aloud at the unbounded outbreak of my childish emotion and my vain entreaty seemed not to be ineffectual. Miriam Süss suddenly raised herself in the bed, as if lifted by a spring, her beautiful face, already touched by the breath of death, was a blue-white, her eyes protruded far out of their sockets ... *but she did not bless me*!... she folded her hands and began in a tremulous but perfectly intelligible voice: 'Lord of the World!... Thou hast sent thy messenger to me, and I must pass into the shadowy realms of death.... I tremble before Thee, O Lord and Judge! for I have sore sinned, gone sore astray!... Forgive me, O God, Thou that art gracious to all, and pardoneth iniquity and sins; I have bitterly repented, made large atonement.... and that all men may know, that my repentance is perfect and sincere, I will now in the last moment of my life, openly and loudly confess before thee my husband and these worthy men the whole enormity of my inexpiable guilt.... *I broke my marriage vows to thee.... and my son Gabriel is not thy son....*' Blume! what I felt at that moment, poor human speech is incapable of expressing.... Grief, passion, woe, torment--put together in one conception all the notions that these words embrace; multiply them by thousands,--and you will still have no idea of that which coursed quivering through my broken heart,--With one blow, with one single, mighty, well-aimed blow, an infinite filial love was driven out of my breast, and the blackest hate filled me, a hate, well founded and inextinguishable. Had I lived a thousand lives and every moment of my life committed a deadly sin, yet *if there is a divine justice....* all the iniquity of my life would have been atoned for by this too woeful moment. At the very time when I was supplicating with hot tears a blessing from my dying mother--*she betrayed me*, cast me out of the Paradise of my life into never ending torment.... at a time when for her I would have breathed out my life with a smile and in silence under the cruellest tortures, when I would have with joy delivered my soul for her salvation to the everlasting torments of the damned, at *that time my mother betrayed me*!!! 'Mad liar! recall the words! say that an evil spirit has spoken by thy mouth!' I cried in a furious voice, shaking violently her almost inanimate body. 'I cannot, Gabriel, I cannot,' she shrieked, 'pray for me!... Lord of the world! forgive me! be gracious unto me! have pity on me! I have sore sinned.... Oh God! accept my confession and death as atonement! Hear Israel ...' she could say no more, her eyes grew dim--she fell back--a light death sigh heaved her breast--she had ceased to exist.... 'No, dead mother, No,' I cried, 'God will not have compassion upon thee, since thou knewest no compassion for me--I curse thee and thy memory: ...'

I uttered the most fearful maledictions, the most horrible curses--they tore me from my mother's lifeless corpse....

"Joseph Süss Lad sunk speechless at the confession of his guilty wife. When he came to himself he foamed with rage. His guilty wife was dead and the poor deceived man turned the whole weight of his irreconcilable wrath upon my innocent head.--The bond that should have united us to one another was loosed, I was not his son, I was a stranger--oh! far less than a stranger.... He took no time for reflection, and an hour later I stood alone, forsaken, an outcast from the house, that I had hitherto called my home! Thus had one moment, one word, robbed me of father, mother, love, memory, past and future.

"I wandered all the night about the town, I could not wait till morning dawned, and when it came I wished that the darkness of night had endured for ever. Early on new year's day every one went to the synagogue, I, I alone shunned the face of men.... I would not remain in the street, and in the despair of my heart turned my steps towards the dwelling of my early teacher, a sick, bed-ridden old man, obliged even on highest feast-days to perform his devout exercises at home. I found him already sitting up in bed and reading by the light of a lamp. The report of my humiliation had already reached even him, at sight of his once loved scholar he uttered a cry and the bible fell from his trembling hands. Was it chance, was it perhaps that my old teacher, revolving my unhappy situation, had opened at the passage in scripture that applied to it, I know not; but as I bent to pick up the book, my glance fell upon it, the words danced in varied iridescence before my burning eyes, I read the words: 'A bastard shall not enter into the congregation of the Lord.' I felt anew a wild spasm at my heart. Together with the fearful unutterable excitement that had seized me at the shameless confession of that woman, who had carried me in her womb, with the crushing pain of seeing myself so humiliated before the eyes of men; there had also sprung up the melancholy self-tormenting feeling that I owed my existence to a sin, that I had been launched into the world against the will of the Most High, whom I at that time worshipped with boundless reverence: ... But as I once more read those clear and significant words, the words of that scripture which I had hitherto looked upon as binding and sacred--as I read the sentence of the Lord, whom I, bowed to the dust in fulness of faith, had called all-merciful, all-good, all-just--as I read the judgment, that made me, me guiltless of the transgression, miserable--that brought me to naught; T tore out of my lacerated and bleeding heart that blind faith, that could never restore me to bliss, never make me happy, that faith which might never more seem true and sacred to me.... I tore myself free from religion, sweet comfortress, that offered consolation to all but me...."

"It was mid-day. The walls of the city were too confined for me. I went out, and while my former brethren in the faith were praying in God's house, I sat alone in the deep forest, weeping hot bitter tears, tears more agonizing than man had ever wept before! It was a lovely fresh autumnal day, the rays of the sun pierced with deadened heat through the tops of the trees tinted with the yellow hues of autumn, the birds chirped cheerful songs, a soft mild wind breathed through the withering arbour, the deepest peace had dominion around: in me seethed the bitterest deadliest hatred.--I may have sat there for hours plunged in the most melancholy brooding, when I suddenly started up: It flashed across me, like bright lightning in a clear night, that I was not yet lost. Thy loved image, Blume! appeared all at once in liveliest colours before my soul. I still had thee! only thee in the wide world: but still I had thee: what more could I want?" The sentence of Scripture had branded me, my mother had betrayed me, my brethren had rejected me,--but still I had thee, thee, Blume! thou who couldest make up to me for all that, all of it, all. To thee I now transferred the whole wealth of my undivided love! a nameless ardent longing after thee burnt like wild fire in my soul; my love to thee had reached the height of madness. Remembrance of thee had effaced the horrible warning of the immediate past, had averted my gaze from the dark future--to live with thee, Blume! in some remote corner of the world, so sweet a child, my child!... "Blume," said Gabriel, suddenly breaking off with an accent of the most passionate grief.---"Thou mightest have been my guardian angel.... By thee, Blume, I might have been converted again.... Thou hast dealt injuriously with me, thou hast not acted justly.--Blume, if there is a God--hearest thou! I will not believe it, I dare not believe it, but if there is, Blume! at thy hands will my soul be required!... I hurried to Worms--how thy father rejected me with contumely, how I learnt, that as soon as they had received the quickly circulated news, they had instantly betrothed thee to thy father's nephew, thy cousin Aaron,--all that you know.--What I suffered, that you did not know, no! for the honour of humanity I will believe that you did not know it--I insisted on speaking to you alone; I trusted that your father had lied, that you would behave differently to the others, would have compassion upon me, would love me! I waited wistfully for the feast of atonement: I knew, that while the rest were praying in God's temple, you would remain at home with your blind mother. On the afternoon of the festival I crept into your house. Breathless I hurried through the well-known passages and opened the door that led into your mother's room. She was asleep, you were sitting by her bed and praying. I stood on the threshold trembling like an aspen. I thought that with a cry of joy you would throw yourself into my arms, kiss the tears from my eyelids, dry the cold drops of anguish that fell from my forehead. 'Blume,' I cried, 'wilt fly with me? Wilt be my wife?' you were silent. 'You too Blume!'

I cried in inexpressible sorrow, and fell at your feet.... your bosom panted, your lips moved, as though you would speak, but you did not speak, your look fixed itself ghostlike upon me, as if I, innocent and unfortunate, had escaped from hell! I wished to break the dull silence, I sought for words, to move you, to melt the hard marble of thy heart; but I suddenly felt myself seized from behind, your father, your betrothed had returned home to enquire after your mother's health. A wild fury disfigured their faces.... you heard how they insulted and laughed me to scorn, you saw how they cast me forth, mercilessly, pitylessly, as a mangy hound is expelled with kicks; yes you saw it, but said nothing, you did not fall into their arms, ... you did not stand trembling and wringing your hands.... 'Blume,' yelled Gabriel shaking her fiercely by the arm, and a mad fury flashed from his eyes, 'why did you allow that horror to be perpetrated, tell me, woman! why? Why did you give your hand to the man, who so fearfully and undeservedly insulted me, an innocent man,--tell me, why? speak!'"

Blume sobbed violently, she folded her beautiful white hands, her lips moved silently in fervent prayer.

"Blume!" said Gabriel, after a moment's pause, in a dull unsteady voice. "If my deadly enemy, who bears an everlasting hatred to me, who strives with hot desire to drink my heart's blood--if my deadly enemy were to lay at my feet as I on that evening kneeled before thee, I who am steadfast in hate, I who know no pity, should weep hot tears of compassion--and I was not your enemy, I had loved you with a love as infelt and holy as is permitted to a human soul, I would have given the last drop of my heart's blood for one tear from your eyes,--and you, a weak, mild, pitiful woman, would not weep that tear.... You stood there dismayed, but did not keep off those furious one's.... What had I done to you? What was my transgression? Had not I been, to my mother's last breath, devout, noble, self-sacrificing?--Why did you solemnly inter the guilty mother as a contrite penitent, and cast out the innocent son? When I was cast forth from your house, Blume! when the last cable of my hope snapped there:--then I swore in my soul, a fearful undying vengeance: ... I love not men, I hate you Jews, but the most burning hate that man, or perhaps hell is capable of, I bear against thy mother, thy husband, and far beyond all in my heart against thee."

"Then slay me," cried Blume hastily, "and leave my husband, my mother, leave all in peace! let the whole weight of your anger fall on my head, slay me, Gabriel, but spare the others...."

The tiny sleeper on her arms awoke again and stretched its hands smiling towards its mother. Blume shuddered and broke into loud sobbing: "No, Gabriel, slay me not, let me live, see me at thy feet,"--she cast herself upon her knees--"let me live, I supplicate not for myself, by the Almighty God, not for my own sake;--but look at this innocent babe, its father is far away, it has only its mother, could you be responsible for depriving it of its mother? You do not know what a mother feels for her child."

"Hush, Blume, and stand up!" cried Gabriel, pulling the kneeling woman up from the ground, and the veins in his forehead swelled high: "are you mad? Do you think I shall murder a defenceless woman? be composed, I shall not slay thee.... That is not the revenge I shall take."

Both were silent. Blume opened the window, she looked whether a light was still burning in the lecture-room, a faint glimmer shot from the windows of the distant edifice, she felt relieved by the knowledge that men were still awake there! A cold wind blew through the room, neither Gabriel or Blume observed it, only the child shivered in its mother's arms.

"You have suffered much," so Blume broke the long painful silence.

"You have fallen off from the faith of your fathers? You are ..., you were...."

Blume knew not what she said, but this silence of the grave was mortal to her, she was constrained to speak, and almost involuntarily emitted these words from her lips.

"From the faith of my fathers!" re-echoed Gabriel; "you choose your words well, each is a poisoned arrow and barbed--have I then forsaken the faith of my fathers? Do I forsooth know my father? For ten years have I sought him, and thee," he continued thoughtfully, "thee have I found,--shall I ever discover him, whom perhaps--and supposing I did find him," said Gabriel after a long silence, inwardly communing, and rather as addressing himself, "would the voice of nature, as silly men declare, conquer? Full of infinite love should I fling myself into my father's arms, or should I be possessed with an unspeakable hatred against the faithless traitor, who was perhaps wantoning in luxury, when his child, loaded with insult and scorn, was cast out from the threshold of that house that he had for twenty years called home! If he proves such a man, if he has forgotten me, if he has never been mindful of the unhappy one whom to his everlasting misery he tossed out into the wide desolate world; if he proves like the mother, who even on her death-bed betrayed her child, if he should prove such, and I do find him, Blume: I shall gloriously conclude my wretched existence with a parricide."

Blume shuddered. Gabriel threw himself into a chair and hid his face with both hands.

"But if it is not so, supposing it otherwise," he began again after a long pause, in the course of which the foaming billows of his wrath had sunk, "if the apparition in my youth was a truth and no deception, if his tears did indeed once bedew the face of his child, if my father has been pining in infinite sorrow for his long lost son, if his heart has been sighing after me with the same strange emotion as sometimes in hours of quiet rises convulsively in the depths of my soul, if racked by repentance and the stings of conscience he has been seeking me mad with grief.... if I should find him thus, though he were the meanest on earth, the wretchedest beggar to whom one flings a morsel of bread--and stood before me in that condition--Blume! I have often declared, and now repeat, by my troth, and knightly honour! I should fold him lovingly in my arms.... and though it were the last moment of my life, my last breath--my last, yea dying breath should be a loud Hallelujah."

Gabriel stopped suddenly, Blume too had for some time been listening. Out of the bushes in a distant corner of the graveyard, on the gusts of a favouring wind, sounds of lamentation came born to the ears of both of them. Each for a time had accepted what was heard as a deception to be accounted for by the fearful excitement of the moment; but the sounds, at first dying away with a hollow echo, came nearer:

"My Son, my Son;" it rung now clearer and clearer in their ears, "my much loved only child--where art thou? Come to me, thou dear one.... thou wert born in sin, but I love thee in spite of all! for in truth you are my only son! Where can I find thee? could I find thee in heaven, I would seek thee there; could I find thee far over the sea, I would seek thee there.--Where art thou, thou that wert conceived in sin, thou that art so near to my heart? approach me and let us crave mercy at my father's grave, perhaps God will have compassion on me, will pardon me!... Oh! if my son but lives and I may see him again: then, then would I die!..."

The clock on a neighbouring tower tolled midnight, a wind sprung up, and sighed over the wide desolate space of the graveyard.... the clang of the clock, the rustling of the wind drowned the words which again died away in the distance. Gabriel had become deadly pale. He stepped to the window, and gazed for a long while down: but saw nothing. "It was an illusion," he said softly, quickly recovering himself by a wonderful mental effort--"my sharp glance detects nothing in the wide, and snow-covered space--and the dead have no voice."

Blume shivered, she did not dare announce that she too had heard the ghostly cry from the graveyard. Gabriel stared fixedly before him, sunk in gloomy brooding. Blume tried to read his soul. She had never seen him since that fateful day of the feast of atonement. He, who had once loved her, who had once clung with the perfect fresh strength of youth to his faith, to humanity, to his people, to justice, had become a changed man. Branded by holy scripture, which human wisdom can never quite interpret, betrayed by his mother whom he idolized, driven from her presence, cast forth from the society of his brethren--his soul was filled with hate. But even his hate she was unable to fathom. When he had entered, she feared that he would rob her of her child, that he would slay herself--that he would not do so, was now clear--but she dared not yet be tranquil, for he had declared that he hated her, that he would be revenged upon her. In pitiful sorrow she gazed motionless at his lips, at every movement of which her blood again ran cold: though his silence seemed to her yet more horrible. Once more one of those long and oft-recurring pauses had intervened, that seemed to Blume to last an eternity. Her unspeakable oppression was intensified by the profound impression caused by the singular incident that had just occurred, by astonishment at Gabriel who seemed by force of will to have soon banished it from his soul.

"Gabriel," implored Blume, "I pray thee, speak, break this weird silence, it is awful! say what thou wilt, go on with your story."

"Dost thou consider Blume! thy silence was once awful to me too.... once thou hadest no word of pity, no look of compassion for a poor innocent martyr, and I languished for a word of love.--Had my grandfather then still continued to live at Cologne perhaps.... I do not know, but perhaps he, he alone, would have taken me to his arms. But the fearful tidings, that branded his daughter, his grandson, gave his name a prey to the scornful, and blighted his dearest hopes, threw the old man on a bed of death. I arrived two days after his funeral at Cologne. Every one shunned me, my misfortune was known to all my brethren in the faith.

"I took possession, as heir, of my grandfather's immense property. I was no longer attached by any tie to this life, all that I had loved, I was constrained to hate, that which had once been true and holy to me, now seemed to me lying and false, I was the unhappiest man on earth! I broke with my whole past life, I would have none of it live on within me, except the remembrance of my unmerited humiliation, that fanned the hot flame of my revenge with undiminished fury.... I sought by some overt act to prove that I had become a changed man. In the cathedral at Aix-la-chapelle I abjured the old faith, and swore enmity in my heart against all those that clave to it.... As I came out of the church a crowd of people had assembled to gape at the new convert. I did not lift my eyes; but felt that the odious looks of all were fixed upon me. I hurried through the press, and sought to gain a side street that led to my dwelling. The crowd that accompanied me fell off one by one, and at last I heard the step of but one solitary person behind me, who followed me obstinately to the door of my house. I did not look round, but as I was about to step into the house, I felt myself seized by the cloak. 'What do you want?' I asked of the importunate fellow, a beggar in the dress of a poor Jew. 'Nothing,' replied he, with the wandering gaze of madness, 'nothing, except to tell you, that you have done wrong.... Thou hast forsaken thy Father in heaven.... and a good child seeks his father, even though he has prepared sorrow for him.... There is no greater grief than when father and son seek and cannot find one another!...' The maniac ran quickly away: but his words, burnt into my soul like kindled sparks.--I did not know my father! my mother had died without naming his name.--The high reputation for virtue which she had enjoyed during her lifetime, had not permitted the faintest doubt to rest upon her, and even if I had ventured to induce my brethren to make any revelations, my inquiries would have been vain. I had as yet been too stunned to think of my unknown father; but now, with the wild thirst for vengeance on you all, was associated a feeling, so singular, so wonderful, that I can never describe it. At one moment I was inflamed with unutterable hate against the unknown author of my days, at another I felt myself more mildly disposed, and a profound longing took possession of my torn heart. At one moment I believed myself convinced that he had forgotten me, and revelled with undisturbed and cheerful mind in earthly happiness, while his son succumbed before a woeful affliction; at another I hoped that he, who had never betrayed me, who had never for years enforced his paternal authority, had omitted to do so by reason of his inextinguishable love for me. A tormenting, frequently rapid succession of emotions took powerful hold on my heart; but from that moment a desire was born within me to find my father, were it to demand fearful reckoning of him, or were it to fall reconciled into his fatherly arms!

"Three days later I received intelligence that they had wedded you to your betrothed. You were in a great hurry, and your grandfather's death could not deter you from your hasty resolution. Thou, my ardently beloved adored bride, gavest thy hand to him who had disgracefully mis-used me as I lay on my knees in supplication before thee!... The marriage was solemnized at Worms, while I in Aix was languishing in maddest grief!--My determination to be avenged remained firm and immovable, but I was as yet too weak, too powerless to carry it into effect!"

Gabriel ceased, pressed both hands to his burning forehead and went on, after a long pause, passionlessly almost calmly.

"I was restless and changeable, I knew not whither to turn my steps, nor what to set about. War was kindled in a part of Germany, but I did not care about it, I was indifferent to it. I wandered in wild fury from city to city, from village to village; and found nowhere peace and rest. I was often forced to rise in the middle of the night and travel further: an irresistible power seemed to urge me on. One stormy winter's night I had arrived at a small town in the district of Juliers, and intended to pass the night there: but sleep fled my wearied eyes, about midnight I arose and had my horse saddled. My servant resolutely refused to go on in the fearful storm, people dissuaded me from continuing my journey, the roads were unsafe.--Nothing could restrain me, some impulse drove me abroad!... I may have ridden for two hours objectless, when I suddenly heard a report of firearms. I rode in the direction whence the noise came, and saw by the light of the full moon, that momentarily appeared through an opening in the wind-riven clouds, a group of horsemen engaged at a short distance in a fierce struggle. I almost involuntarily spurred my horse to a swifter pace, and first held rein when close to the angry fight. This was an unequal one. Five horsemen, manifestly the aggressors, formed a half circle round a tall and knightly form. Enveloped in a white mantle, his head protected by an open dragoon's helmet, the man who was attacked was obliged at the moment of my arrival to make head alone against the superior number, for his attendant had fallen shortly before, wounded by a pistol-shot. I remained for a moment an inactive spectator. Two corpses and two masterless steeds on the side of the assailants proved beyond a doubt that the White-mantle and his companion had made good use of their fire-arms; but now that this last had been put hors-de-combat the other was fully occupied in parrying the thrusts of the attacking party. The moon threw its pale light on the White-mantle, who, with lips fast pressed, flashing eye and steady hand covered himself against every assault, and wielded his mighty sword with almost superhuman strength. The weapons clashed, other wise there was a profound stillness. I approached in rear of the assailants. When he who was sore pressed saw me, a ray of hope seemed to flit over his pale noble features; but no sound escaped his lips. My arrival altered the position of affairs. Two of the horsemen wheeled round and presented their pistols at me. 'Brandenburgian or Imperialist?' they cried.--'It's all the same to me,' was my honest answer. One of my interrogators now turned about, and aimed steady and sure at the head of the White-mantle. At that moment my full sympathy was aroused for the man whose life was threatened.

"He was forsaken, alone against many:--without analysing my motive, driven by some inner impulse without even knowing to what party he belonged, I drew the pistols from my holster, and shot down the man who had taken aim. 'Receive my thanks, Saviour in the hour of need, I will never forget you,' cried White-mantle, raising himself, as if endued with fresh strength, high in his saddle, and directing against one of his surprised opponents a blow so mighty that he fell lifeless to the ground. We were now two against three--the White-mantle was saved--with a wonderful inimitable, caracole he placed his horse by my side. I had not time to discharge my second pistol, for our opponents, well skilled in arms, pressed us with redoubled impetuosity. I tore the sword from my side and fought with that boundless untamed fury that filled my heart. The hot fight did me good, I did not feel the blood, trickling from my arm, but on a sudden out of the neighbouring thicket a ball whistled by my ear, I fell wounded.... Whitemantle supported me with one arm, with the other still kept brandishing his mighty weapon. At that instant I heard the tramp of horses, but closed my eyes and lost consciousness. Eight days later when I recovered my senses I found myself to my astonishment in a handsome apartment in Juliers.... I was lying in bed--I learnt that the warrior, whose life I had saved, was the Imperialist General, Count Ernest of Mannsfield, Margrave of Castelnuovo and Bortigliere. Brandenburgian horsemen had laid in wait for him, when he rashly enough, accompanied only by his lieutenant, had set out on his way back to the city. The ball which had struck me, was fired by some sharpshooters from Neuberg, who had come to the aid of the Brandenburgers: but the report of fire-arms had at the same instant brought up some Imperial dragoons whose arrival had settled the small skirmish in our favour. They told me that Mannsfield was ardently desirous of offering his thanks to me for the unexpected help, and when I declared that I now felt myself well and strong enough to receive his visit, some moments afterwards he entered my room. Mannsfield was at that time twenty years old. He was a tall powerful man; his extraordinarily pale earnest face with pointed Spanish beard and mustachios was framed with dark waving locks, his large eyes gazed feelingly at me, he held out his hand. 'I thank thee, Brother,' he said with emotion, and each of his words made a deep impression upon my poor heart, void of love.--'Thou hast saved my life, I will never--may God help me--forget thee! You were ignorant whom you succoured, you offered--as a good soldier should--a saving hand, not to the Count Mannsfield, not to the Imperial Marshal, no, to the man, to the hard pressed worn-out unknown soldier! no oath bound you, what you did for me had its source only in the free will of your noble soul....'

"Blume! you had all rejected me, I stood alone in the wide world, my heart, that could love so warmly, so boundlessly, was desolate and bleeding. Each word of Mannsfield's dropped balsam upon the wounds of my soul: an emotion, so profound, as could only be excited in me at a time when still credulous and undeceived, I dared live for a sweet delusion, thrilled through me; my whole heart expanded to his words, I pressed the hand of the noble soldier, and hot tears rolled from my eyes. 'Now if you are strong enough, and talking does not try you,' continued Mannsfield, 'let me learn the name of my saviour. What is thy escutcheon, where is thy home?'

"Drops of agony stood on my forehead. Once more the past moved in swift flight over my soul, all seemed to me a confused dream! I fought a hard fight with myself; chance had led me to a powerful grateful friend, could I venture to narrate to him frankly and unconstrainedly my life's history? Had I not reason to fear that the renowned hero, the General, the Emperor's favourite would turn scornfully from me? from me, a renegade Jew, an outcast of his brethren, a man branded from his birth? Mannsfield remarked my hesitation. 'I will not urge you,' he continued after a pause of surprise: 'perhaps a mystery hangs over your name--I am sorry, but be you what or who you will you will ever remain dear to me--a thought suddenly flashed across him. Perhaps you are a Protestant? perhaps an adherent of the Union?' he exclaimed, 'ah how little you know Mannsfield! By God Almighty--be you who you will--you are prized by and dear to me.... Shall I speak to you in confidence? I am at the bottom of my heart not averse to the Protestantism, which I now do battle against under the standard of my glorious Imperial master:--But I am rivetted to the illustrious House of Austria by a bond of gratitude: I was brought up at the Court of my godfather the Archduke Ernest; I have to thank my Imperial lord and master for all that I am, and why should I conceal from you, my preserver, that for which I have so often been compelled to blush, and what half Germany knows.... I was not born in lawful wedlock, and I only owe it to the especial favour and grace of the monarch, that he permits me to enjoy the name and rank of my father, that he has legitimised me, that he has pledged his Imperial word as soon as the war which we are now waging is over, to invest me with all my father's possessions. Mannsfield's words made a tremendous impression upon me. Blind chance had wonderfully guided me. That the birth of this man, whom I had saved, who was soliciting my friendship and love should have been first legitimised by the absolute command of the Emperor, that I had saved him while my heart was overflowing with hate, that he, the brave lion-hearted hero who had staked his life thousands of times for his Emperor, his colours, his glory, laid such stress upon it, all this had such a decisive influence upon me, that I broke the deep silence, which I had firmly intended to preserve, and revealed to Mannsfield my whole past history. Mannsfield listened to me with the warmest infelt sympathy. 'You are alone in the world,' he said, after I had ended, in the harmonious accents of his powerful voice, 'you have saved my life.... Your secret shall for ever be preserved in my breast--will you be my brother?' Mannsfield gazed at me out of his deep dark eyes so cordially, so lovingly. My heart beat as if it would burst. Mannsfield despised me not, Mannsfield did not hold out to me only a poor common oblation of compassion: no, he offered me all his great heart--could I refuse the too-bountiful present? Tears, that rolled from my eyes, were my only answer. We sealed the compact with a long fraternal embrace.--Eight days afterwards I was entirely recovered, and was presented to the assembled officers as a new companion in arms at a banquet given in Mannsfield's honour. They had named me at my baptism Gottfried. But God was no longer in my heart, peace was never in my soul, I banished both from my name, and called myself Otto Bitter. I took service in the Imperial army under that perfectly unknown name.--The vast wealth that I had inherited from my grandfather supplied the means of equipping at my own cost some troops of cavalry, in return for which I was appointed to their command. Fortune, which favoured my arms, in conjunction with Mannsfield's inexhaustible affection for me, quickly promoted me from step to step and allowed me to take conspicuous rank in the army under Arch-duke Leopold which was detailed to operate against the Unionists in the Cleves-Juliers district. The continuance of the war had fully occupied me, but spite of the fact that my past history was to remain a mystery to every one except Mannsfield, I had succeeded in obtaining tidings of thee and thine. I was indeed far from you, but in spirit I stood ever near you, I never lost sight of you for a moment--after a series of battles the Protestant Union at length concluded a peace with the Emperor, in order to oppose their whole force to the newly formed Catholic confederacy, the League. I was free, I wished to hurry to Worms, to appear before thee and thine, and settle accounts with you--but a new and unexpected turn in the fortunes of my friend Mannsfield hindered me. Mannsfield had confidently expected that the Emperor at the end of the campaign would have invested him with the possessions of his deceased father who had been Stadtholder in Luxembourg. The war of succession in Juliers and Cleves was over; the complication in Alsace arranged: Mannsfield had rendered the Emperor substantial services; he had shed his blood upon the field of battle; he had squandered his rich maternal heritage in warlike armaments, without demanding compensation for it: it was only through Mannsfield's zeal, through his high military talents and spirit of self-sacrifice that the Imperial General-in-chief the Arch-duke Leopold had been enabled to make head successfully against a superior force. Mannsfield now applied for the desired investment, but was shamefully refused. His proud spirit could not brook the slight which was inflicted on him, he retired from the Imperial service, and devoted his zeal and victorious sword to the evangelical Union. It was perfectly indifferent to me, for whom or what I fought.--A firm indissoluble bond of friendship united me to Mannsfield, I could not hesitate a moment, I ranged myself by Mannsfield's side. Victory was tied to Mannsfield's standard. I was his truest and best companion in arms, the fortune of war was favourable to me; loved by Mannsfield, idolised by the troops I now became the first officer in his army.--In the meanwhile a persecution of the Jews had broken out in Frankfurt stirred up by Vettmilch,

Gerngross and Schopp. The Jewish quarter was plundered and wasted, the life of your brethren threatened. The rabble at Worms wished to follow the example of Frankfurt and a pretext was easily found. Your family, the Rottenbergs, had some, I do not doubt well grounded claim, against a Frankfurt patrician; he died, and his son who had been admitted to the rights and privileges of a citizen at Worms found it most convenient to get rid of the obligation into which his father had entered, first by disputing the demand as usurious, but afterwards the receipt for the debt as forged. The honour, property, safety of your family were all equally endangered. The workmen at Worms, friendly to a hasty course as it was a question of using violence against the Jews, looked upon the private suit as a public concern and demanded from the Imperial Chamber at Spires the immediate expulsion of all Jews from Worms. They were sent back and ordered to follow the usual course of justice in reference to your affair. But the Imperial judges were stern and just, and there was no doubt therefore, that you would win your cause. The trades, irritated to the highest degree by the failure of their plan, demanded that you should make a sacrifice of your claim, and moreover in order to save the honour of their fellow citizen should declare the proofs to be forged. You made up your minds to lose the sum, which was a considerable one, but no one could persuade you to make a false dishonourable confession. Vain was the pressure of the workmen, vain the prayers of your brethren in Worms, who were blind enough not to detect the clumsy artifice and believed in their simplicity that the artisans of Worms would be appeased by this declaration, and undertake no further hostilities against the Jews. You remained firm and in the week before Easter the wild storm broke loose. The magistrates, though with the best intentions, too feeble to protect you, were obliged to look on bewildered and inactive, while the Jews were expelled, their ancient synagogues demolished their burial ground desecrated.--It was only through the immense exertions of the Bishop, who only arrived in Worms late in the evening of that hapless day, that the wild fury of the populace was at length bridled. A general plunder was prevented, too late however for you, against whom the popular hatred had first vented itself. Your house was entirely demolished, you were plundered, your father was roughly handled. You had only escaped a certain death by speedy flight. Your father died from the effects of the fright and ill-usage that he had experienced.--The Frankfurt rebels were subdued by force of arms. An Imperial commissioner punished the guilty and the Jews returned in triumph to the city. In Worms also the insurgents soon surrendered to the Imperial troops, the Jews were recalled and honourably re-instated in their ancient residences. But you never returned. The community of Worms maintained that the calamity was attributable to your obstinacy, that much worse might have happened, that you should have sacrificed your honour and pride to the common-weal. The community excluded you from the midst of them. Poor and wretched, concealing your shame under an assumed name, you were forced to seize the beggar's staff and start on a wide uncertain wandering. The punishment was hard, but you had deserved it for your behaviour to me!"

Blume had again silently listened to Gabriel without interrupting him. It seemed to her almost as if he took pleasure in the pleasing broad circumstantiality of the story as he told it. As if he took a pleasure in embodying in living sounding words his whole past, that he must for years have kept sealed in his heart. As he spoke of that time when he was far from her, he seemed to become more calm. A mild conciliatory spirit seemed to come over him, when he referred to Mannsfield and the firm bond of friendship that united their hearts to one another. When he spoke of the persecution of the innocent Jews in Frankfurt and Worms it seemed to her as if love for his former brethren was not yet altogether dead in him, as if a feeling of compassion still stirred in the depths of his almost inscrutable soul. She already yielded to the delusive hope that Gabriel was only come to forgive her and had only wished to give her a fright by calling up the memory of the past. The earnest warning was to serve only to annihilate her by the full weight of his magnanimity;--but when he once more probed with rough hand her bleeding wounds, when he once more spoke of punishment, thought of retaliation, she again sunk down, covering her beautiful face with both hands. Gabriel did not notice it. "From that moment I lost all trace of you. I had joined fortune with my friend Mannsfield, and was hurried from one end of Germany to the other. Everywhere I looked sharply out for thee. If I came into the neighbourhood of a Jewish community, I often exchanged armour and helm for cloak and cap, in order to obtain admittance into it as a travelling student that I might search thee out. When my disguise could not be kept secret from those about me, a silly foolish love-affair with a Jewish girl served as an excuse for it. My inquiries were in vain, but I doubted not, I was convinced that I must some day find you.... We were just on the point of hurrying off to the assistance of the Duke of Savoy, a member of the Union, when suddenly the flame of war was kindled in Bohemia. The duke no longer required reinforcement, it was a matter of indifference to Mannsfield in what quarter he waged war on behalf of Protestantism against the Emperor: we marched therefore at the request of the Bohemian states, who took us into their pay, to Bohemia. Our arrival was immediately illustrated by a victory, we took the strong and disaffected city of Pilsen. The Emperor was exasperated to the highest pitch by the loss of this loyal city, and Mannsfield and I his chief officer, were put under the ban of the Empire. Meanwhile the Bohemians had elected the Palatine Frederick their king. The selection was an unfortunate one. Frederick appointed Anhalt and Hohenlohe commanders-in-chief of his army and Mannsfield remained at Pilsen at a distance from head-quarters in order to escape serving under both of them. We found ourselves badly off. Pay and support, as well from the Union as from the Palatine, failed. Mannsfield was obliged to keep the army on foot without money. To fill up the measure of our misfortunes, that portion of the country in which we were encamped was attached to the Imperial party and we were surrounded by spies.--We were obliged to observe the greatest watchfulness and every one, who afforded the slightest ground for suspecting him of being a spy, was arrested and strictly examined. A travelling Jew was once detained; it was known that the Jews of Prague were zealous and faithful partisans of the imperial faction, it was not impossible, that he was a spy. He was brought before me, I recognised him immediately. He had formerly been with me for some time at the high school at Frankfurt, I had seen him too several times at Worms. My altered situation made me quite irrecognisable. To his astonishment I asked him if he knew anything of your whereabouts, and he reluctantly confessed to me that he had caught a glimpse of the long lost woman in Prague, but that you had timidly shunned any meeting. The poor student had not had the remotest intention of acting as a spy and only wished to travel to Fürth. I dismissed him, unenlightened, but with a munificent present. It had been suggested long before that I should undertake a journey to Prague in order to petition the king for the arrears of pay, and to talk over a common plan of campaign with Anhalt. I had hitherto put off the troublesome business, but when I learnt that you were at Prague, I declared myself at once ready for the journey. I arrived here and after three days of ineffectual exertion with king and council, I resolved to stay here till I had discovered you.... I had taken up my quarters in the house of an armourer who had once served as sergeant-major in my regiment.--He had become incapable of further service, and had joined the great swarm of foreigners who had come to Prague with the Palatine. He had always been devoted to me and I could reckon upon his fidelity and secrecy..... I once more pretended a love-affair, when I exchanged the dress of a General for that of a student. I went into the Jews-town and assumed the family name of Mar. By a fortunate coincidence I found a lodging in the house of the upper-attendant of the synagogue, Reb Schlome Sachs. Situated outside of the gate of the Ghetto it was peculiarly adapted for the double purpose of my residence here. Immediately on my entrance into the Ghetto too I had, in a really inexplicable way, found favour in the eyes of a usually reserved and maniacal old man, and I felt myself, without being able to give a reason for it, stirred by an unwonted feeling of sympathy for him--perhaps, as I was afterwards obliged to admit, on the ground that his strange madness reminded me of the misfortune of my own life. I was a stranger in the Jewish community of Prague: you lived here quiet and retired under an assumed foreign name. Every enquiry among your co-religionists gave occasion for a well founded suspicion against me, rendered a discovery of my true relation to them possible. It was therefore only through the intermediation of the lunatic that I could hope to discover you: but when I sought him for the second time in his dwelling, I found it shut up, and since the day of my arrival I have never been able to obtain a sight of him. But as I knew that he communicated with nobody, I could at least allege my acquaintance with him, which was concluded in open street, as an excuse for my frequent absence from home, and my landlord Reb Schlome Sachs often believed me to be sympathetically seated by the madman while I was engaged in negotiating with the king and field-marshal about pay in arrear, or campaigns that had miscarried. I ranged through the streets of the Jews-town assiduously, but never saw you. I was almost in despair of finding you here, when a lucky chance led you yesterday to meet me at the threshold of the bathhouse, exactly *yesterday*, when by a concurrence of events I became master of your destiny. Yesterday, after a martyrdom of ten years, I found thee; today I stand before thee...."

Blume had again been listening to Gabriel without uttering a word. He had again, either in self-forgetfulness or mastering his unbridled passion by an astonishing exercise of mental strength been addressing her in the accents of former years. Blume gave way as before to a consoling hope, but Gabriel's last words dispelled all her illusions.

"What do you want of me?" she cried again, lifting herself up and bending involuntarily over the cradle of her child. "What do you want of me? Speak it out, Gabriel! and torture me not to death with protracted anguish...."

"Thou askest what I want?" shouted Gabriel with flashing glance, and his voice sounded like the growling of a thunderstorm: "what I want? *thee!* thou wert mine, Blume! from thy birth up thou wert destined for me, the covenant which our parents had concluded for us, we confirmed by the bond of love--*thou* hast loosened the beautiful bond of love, and now Hate binds me to thee! If it is no longer the heaving of thy voluptuous bosom, if it is no longer the waving of thy dark luxurious tresses, if it is no more the flashing of those beautiful love-kindling eyes, or those rosy budding lips which rapturously attract me to thee.... Why then it is the sweet stupifying poison of revenge! you rejected me, you trampled upon me, ... for a sin that I never committed--if the curse of that sin bears heavily upon my wretched tainted existence--I will at least taste the sweetness of the sin.... I will...."

Blume was for a moment motionless from horror, then seized her child impetuously, opened the window and leaned far out of it, as though to call for help--Gabriel seized her by the arm.

"Be still, Blume," he said, "be not afraid, I shall do nothing by brute force. Thou wilt have time for consideration, and thou wilt throw thyself supplicatingly into my arms.... I give you a week for consideration.... but I believe your resolution will be taken sooner.... Eight days hence, Sunday the eighth of November--it is exactly the anniversary of our betrothal--I shall be with you by midnight.... Wilt thou be mine?"

God-forsaken! screamed Blume beside herself with fury, with flaming face and sparkling eyes: "dost thou desire *that* of me, of me, the wife of another, the devout Jewess, the faithful wife, the tender mother? Yes my resolve is quickly made...."

"It is because you are the wife of another man," interrupted Gabriel, "that I do desire it.--*Wert thou free,* and lying at my feet in all the infinite beauty that neither sorrow nor wretchedness can rob you of, wert thou imploring one glance of love--I should spurn thee from me, as thou didst spurn me,--but the bond of wedlock enchains thee! thou shalt sin, thy hard marble heart shall learn to know the bitter torments of remorse,--and it is because thou art a faithful wife, because thou lovest thy husband, because thou wouldest preserve a father for his child that I expect the fulfilment of my wish."--He drew a packet from his breast-pocket, it contained some small manuscript parchment rolls and a sheet of paper; he handed them in silence to the woman who trembled with rage and grief.

"That is my husband's writing!" shrieked Blume, "those are the texts that he has copied.... God! there is one of my letters. How did you come into possession of these writings? Where is my husband? speak!"

"Read," answered Gabriel, and held out to her Mannsfield's letter which he had received the day before from the ensign. Blume devoured the writing eagerly, but when she came to the last lines, she tottered and was obliged to steady herself by the arm of the chair. The characters danced before her eyes.... "I cannot read it," she said, "do thou read!"

Gabriel read:

"With regard to the above mentioned Jew, whom my outposts arrested, I think that he is innocent. I was obliged to exercise all my authority to prevent his being torn in pieces by the exasperated soldiery, or hanged on the nearest tree; even some of the officers voted for his death. Seeing that the suspicious writings found upon him are according to his own account Hebrew bible-texts and letters from his wife I have sent them to you to be tested, and your report as to the contents of the writings will give him death or freedom.--The whole affair however is so insignificant that you will have no need to detain Michalowitz respecting it. Only in the event of the Jew being a spy, and the contents of the writings therefore of importance to us, will it be necessary for you to send me advice by a trooper: otherwise on account of the insecurity of the roads to Pilsen do not send me any messenger...."

"Now," cried Blume, hastily, "you see, it is not a cipher, it is only texts and my letters. Have you despatched the messenger who will solve the inauspicious misunderstanding?"

"No! My answer will depend on thine.... Will you eight days hence submit yourself to my will?"

"And if I answer no, what will you do?" asked Blume with the utmost eagerness.

"That answer thou wilt never make," replied Gabriel violently, "thou wilt not compel me to an extreme, to the greatest extremity of all.... So, and so only will I be revenged, Blume, force me to no other, to no bloody vengeance.--I will only repay like by like.... you suffered my heart to break.--Come then, I will be the ever living sting of conscience in thy existence--you let me humiliated, deeply, oh infinitely deeply humiliated.--Come now, I will humiliate thee too. But as for me, I had loved thee, had idolized thee, you repaid my love with hate. I am juster than you--I give you hate for hate!... My resolve is unshakeable!"

Blume stood before Gabriel wringing her hands despairingly.--"No, I cannot believe that you will perpetrate the horrible iniquity of writing to Mannsfield a hellish lie that will cause my husband's death. Consider, Gabriel," she continued almost inaudibly, clasping her hands--"indeed I never injured you, never humiliated, never degraded you. It could not be, I could not be your wife, a higher power placed itself between us, could I, could any one help it? I was innocent, thou wert innocent! Oh Gabriel, thou wouldst only terrify me, thou wilt not write the lie to Mannsfield, is it not so."

"Blume, I am armed against thy entreaty.... for long years have I sought thee, for ten years have I been hatching a thought of vengeance, and now that a wonderful chance throws the reins of your destiny into my hands, shall I let the moment pass by unavailed? Shall thy tears befool me? No, Blume, no, every human life must have some attainable aim.--I had no other than revenge!--My resolve remains unalterable."

"You leave me then but the choice between sin and unutterable woe? You are silent? Gabriel," said Blume after a pause suddenly lifting her lovely head.... "You once loved me, now every spark of that feeling, all sympathy is extinguished in your heart, but I, I pity thee in spite of it!... How low art thou fallen, poor Gabriel!--the proud, high-souled Gabriel, who should have been a guiding light to his people, a giant in intellect, contends with a weak woman, one stricken-down with misery, that with her baby in her arms, makes her trembling supplication before him.... and what kind of victory, what a triumph would he win? He would destroy a poor, wornout woman, by means of an abominable shameless lie, than which humanity can conceive nothing more mean.--Gabriel, at this moment I am more wretched and unhappy than any woman upon earth, but--by God Almighty!--I would not for worlds stand before thee, as thou now standest before me!"--

Gabriel stood with folded arms before Blume. The desperate reckless opposition of the helpless woman, especially the last sorrowful cry of her tortured heart had caused him for a moment, but only for a moment to waver; thoughts like lightning flashed through his soul, feelings that he had long believed dead were stirred up in him, for a moment he entertained a thought of foregoing his vengeance, of forgetting the past, of being re-converted--but he had already gone too far, he had broken with all tradition, the future as he had dreamed of it in his youth, seemed to *him lost for ever*--he could never drawback.--His better genius succumbed, the iniquitous passion conquered.

"My resolution is firm and unshakeable," he said, rapidly preparing to go, as if he himself feared lest he should waver again. "Eight days hence I shall be with you by midnight.--Your husband's fate is in your own hands, ponder upon it till then. My resolve is inflexible!"

He folded himself in his mantle and departed--Blume gave way and sobbed aloud.

Chapter V

The Imperial army advanced without interruption, almost without striking a blow, while Anhalt drew back with his troops to the White-mountain close by Prague. He had barely entrenched his camp, when news arrived that the Duke Maximilian was approaching with his division, and that Boucquoi was following with the remainder of the Imperialists, Anhalt summoned a council of war. Mathias Thurn advised that they should attack the Duke immediately on his approach, before the wearied troops should have time to refresh themselves, and before he could unite himself with Boucquoi. John Bubna, Schlick, Styrum and others supported his proposal, and the Commander-in-chief Prince Anhalt seemed already won over to this view, when Hohenlohe pronounced himself violently against any offensive operation. "We must," he opined, "try and avoid any open battle with a superior force under the command of illustrious generals: the result of battles is uncertain, and a crown is not to be lightly hazarded. We have a strong impregnable position on the heights and the enemy will not venture to assault us." Hohenlohe's plan was adopted, and Mathias Thurn left the council in a state of the highest indignation.--So dawned the morning of the 8th of November, a day destined to have a decisive influence for centuries to come.

Encouraged by Frederick's example who did not allow himself to be the least disturbed in his wonted pleasures and amusements, the people in Prague did not give way to fear, and even in camp on the White-mountain they believed themselves so secure and so little expected an attack, that on that very day--it happed to be Sunday--many of the officers and common soldiers had gone into Prague to see their families.

Gabriel had passed the eight days since his nocturnal visit to Blume in a state of feverish excitement. He greeted the morning of this day, the anniversary of his betrothal, with singular feelings. But one short space of time divided him from the long looked for moment of revenge!

It was forenoon, he was sitting in his room in Reb Schlome Sachs' house sunk in deep thought, and gazing earnestly before him. Feelings most various and violent were preying upon him. He permitted, as he was often wont to do for his own torment, his gaze to hover over his past life. He saw himself a boy, full of peace and faith in the house of his grandfather, in the house of his mother. He saw himself a youth by the side of his grandfather in the presence of his exquisitely lovely bride all glowing with becoming modesty he called to remembrance the golden dreams of his youth, how in blissful hope he purposed to obtain a rapturous world to come by a life dedicated to virtue and faith.... And then how that was all suddenly, oh how suddenly, changed--his dying mother--that feast of atonement when he stood in despair before Blume. And now, now, he was about to take vengeance, fearful vengeance!... He knew that it would be impossible to inflict a more painful wound on Blume, that chaste pure woman, that he could not more deeply degrade her--and yet he did not doubt that the noble faithful woman would make a sacrifice of her honour, her soul's peace to her husband. Sometimes it seemed to him as if the minutes that separated him from midnight were rolling on too quickly, too hurriedly, as if he would enjoy the expectation of the near approaching moment of revenge, more than the moment itself? Generally, however, each second seemed infinitely long, and he could not control his impatience. The thought of his father too, as it always did when he was violently excited, had associated itself with all these recollections, with all these unwonted emotions. Swiftly succeeding feelings of alternate love and hate towards him, the natural desire to learn to know him, perhaps that too which we call the voice of nature, all this together had constantly aroused in his heart an indescribable strange desire. At this instant he doubted whether he would ever find him. One thing that he had striven after for years, he believed that he had attained: but it was impossible that Blume should escape him, he had always been sure, though perhaps years might be consumed in the search, that he must sooner or later discover her. But his father? Of him he knew absolutely nothing, he had not the smallest ground to go upon, not the faintest shadow of a conjecture dawned on him.--Where could he seek him; where could he find *him*?

The hurried opening of the door roused Gabriel suddenly out of the confused chaos of his thoughts, he turned round. Before him stood the boy, the ordinary messenger of the armourer in the Platnergasse.--

"Gracious Sir!" cried the boy, "Captain Schlemmersdorf, is waiting for you at home, he is urgently desirous to speak with you speedily"--Gabriel hesitated.

"Say, you could not find me, young one," he replied after a short reflection: "I wish to remain undisturbed till to-morrow."

"Gracious Sir! It must be about some most weighty matters. The captain was beside himself at not finding you at home, he wished to follow me. I was to tell you, that life, honour, everything was at stake."

Gabriel now rose hastily but with a dissatisfied air and obvious reluctance. Shortly afterwards he had arrived in the manner now well-known to us, at his house in the Marienplatz, where Schlemmersdorf was waiting for him with terrible impatience.

"Where have you been staying so long General?" he cried out to him as he entered, "quick, make haste, take your arms, to horse, to horse.--I pray you haste!"

"What has happened?" enquired Gabriel.

"Nothing pleasant, at least not for the present.... Early this morning the advanced guard of the Bavarian column was seen at the further end of the street. The Prince once again summons the few officers present in camp, to advise whether now at any rate it would not be prudent to receive the advancing troops with an attack: but Hohenlohe absolutely refuses to quit the secure position upon the heights, and whilst he is saying all he can in favour of his view, it is announced that Tilly with his Bavarians has crossed the river by a small bridge without hindrance.--The propitious moment for an attack is lost to us. Duke Maximilian is deploying in the centre his whole well-formed array; Boucquoi, who must have followed close upon the Duke, is taking up a position on the right wing, and we have the entire main-body of the enemy opposed to us.--The Prince, who is expecting every moment to be attacked by the Imperialists, is endeavouring in the greatest haste to range his troops in order of battle. He has despatched Habernfield to the king with a request that he will adjourn the ill-timed banquet that he gives to the English ambassadors, and come to the camp, in order to cheer the low spirits of the troops. Styrum is looking for Mathias Thurn and I have hastened to you--but General! don your armour at once. Why tarry you?"

The General had listened to Schlemmersdorf in silence and in spite of his urgency without the least movement.

"What should I do in camp?" he now enquired.

"A strange question, Sir General," replied Schlemmersdorf excitedly, "as far as one could hastily gather in the camp," he added hurriedly resuming, "you were to take charge of the Hungarian cavalry on the left, instead of Bornemissa, who is lying sick."

"Never, never, Sir Captain," cried the General indignantly, "I will never undertake the command of a detachment unaccustomed to discipline, whose language I do not even know, to whom I could not make my orders intelligible. I am obliged to the Prince for the honour and glory, which might have been obtained with the command.--However, Sir Captain, I cannot be of much use in the camp. I am unacquainted with the state of the army that is drawn up here, I am informed neither as to the strength of the divisions, nor the capacity of their officers; I am entirely ignorant of the plan of proceedings.... Sir Captain, you must yourself allow, it would be an unparalleled event in the history of military operations, if I resolved to accept a command under such circumstances."

Schlemmersdorf could not contest the justice of these observations, he was silent.

"I can therefore render no service outside there," continued Gabriel, "except with my sword, like any other common trooper.... but as the Prince did not choose to invite me to the council, though all the other superior officers here present took part in it, I think he will do very well without an individual officer of Mannsfield's in the battle-field.... Make then my excuses to the Prince, if I stay here, where, precisely to-day urgent business, that admits of no postponement, detains me."

"There is no more urgent duty than honour," burst forth Schlemmersdorf. "I know, General, that you have been badly treated," he added, in a conciliatory tone, "badly treated in many ways, it was wrong of the Prince.... but now you are needed, the Prince summons you, after a victory you shall have full satisfaction...."

Gabriel paced the chamber unquietly in deep emotion; a strange horror that he had never before had a presentiment of, thrilled through him.... that he should that very day be summoned to the battlefield! that very day on the anniversary of his betrothal to Blume, that very day, when he desired to take vengeance, to accomplish his long matured plan!...

Schlemmersdorf was in despair, he was willing to make any concession to gain his object. "General," he said at length stepping close up to Gabriel, "time presses, resolve quickly whilst we are here idly babbling away the time, the Imperialists are perhaps assaulting our lines. This day may decide the fate of Frederick's crown, of Bohemia. Consider; it would be an eternal ineffaceable blot upon your name, if you withdrew at the commencement of a battle.--What would your own age, what would even your friend Mannsfield say?"

Schlemmersdorf had touched Gabriel's weak point. His honour as a soldier and Mannsfield's esteem were his highest possessions. Regard for his honour, and a wild thirst for battle drew him into the field, and yet he on the other hand felt himself chained fast to Prague by brazen bonds.--He had looked death in the face unmoved a thousand times, but to-day, just to-day, so near the goal.... to perish to-day on the battle-field, perhaps to die unavenged, perhaps to die without having retaliated the unspeakable woe that had stricken him, perhaps to die without having achieved one single aim.... that was a thought that filled him with fearful unutterable dismay. It seemed to him as if he must strain every nerve to preserve his life for his revenge, for this night--a discord full of torment rent his heart. For a moment he remained undecided, but when Schlemmersdorf wrapped his cloak about him and without a word of farewell turned his back contemptuously upon him and stepped towards the door, he made a sudden resolution, "I go with you, Schlemmersdorf!" he exclaimed, "go with you ... but I will not fall to-day!"--Schlemmersdorf looked in Gabriel's face with surprise. He knew that it was no expression of mere cowardice that escaped him; but time was too precious for further enquiries, he urged him to make all haste, and shortly afterwards the two were spurring at full speed through the Strahower gate towards the camp. Outside the town they encountered Styrum who had gone in vain quest for Mathias Thurn. *Mathias Thurn was not to be found that day.*

The two hosts were drawn up opposite one another. The Imperial-Bavarian army, over 30,000 strong, was in good order and eager for battle. The Bohemian, scarcely numbering 20,000, was surprised, and in spite of the favourable ground which it occupied was drawn up in a great hurry by Anhalt without any fixed principle. The Prince had brought up all the artillery that he had on to the heights that covered his right wing.--This therefore, commanded by the young Prince Anhalt, was ranged in the line of its own fire, the trajectory of which would pass over its head. Hohenlohe commanded the centre under Anhalt, Bornemissa who had had himself carried to the field in spite of his illness, the left.--The Duke himself commanded the Imperial army in chief, under him Lichtenstein the centre, Tilly the left, Boucquoi, who in spite of the wound that he had received at Rakonitz was again on horse, the right wing.

It was a beautiful fresh winter's day. The Imperialists seemed for some time to be in doubt whether they should advance. At length, between twelve and one o'clock in the afternoon, the two lines of which the extreme wings were made up, set themselves in motion, and pushed forward with drums rolling and loud shouting. Anhalt at once commenced a cannonade from all his guns, but they were pointed too high, and the balls passed far over the heads of the Imperialists without killing even a single man. The right wing of the Bohemians was now impetuously attacked and thrown back: but young Anhalt, supported by Bubna and young Thurn, broke suddenly (according to the enemies' own account) like thunder and lightning in amongst the Imperial cavalry, and his extraordinarily fierce onset in spite of the most obstinate, heroic resistance forced it slowly to give ground. The Imperialists lost three standards, and Captain Preuner was taken prisoner. Victory seemed inclining towards Frederick's side. But at this decisive moment reinforcements arrived for the hard pressed Imperialists. Godfrey of Pappenheim came up with his cuirassiers just in time to prevent young Anhalt's further advance. At sight of the youthful sparkling hero the Imperialists again stood firm, and a terrible hand to hand contest ensued. For a quarter of an hour the fate of the battle in this portion of the field was in suspense.--At that moment the three young men, Gabriel, Schlemmersdorf and Styrum reached the White-mountain. Gabriel had only one personal friend, John Bubna, upon the field. He was on the right wing and thither Gabriel turned his fiery steed. His discontent vanished at sight of the battle-field. The hot fight, the blast of the trumpets, the rattle of musketry, the thunder of cannon, all this made him for a moment forgetful of his resolution. Thus had he often stood at Mannsfield's side. On the battle-plain he had won for himself a new name, respected and terrible. His lust of combat was kindled to a wild heat, he drew his sword, spurred his horse to a mad gallop, and flew swift as an arrow over the level ground that separated him from the field of battle.

"Ah, thou here, young friend!" cried the elder Bubna who had withdrawn for a moment from the thickest pressure, to staunch the blood that was flowing from a flesh-wound.--"That's right of you to come, the sight of you has a wonderfully strengthening effect upon me. How fares it with the other wing?"

"I do not know, Bubna," replied Bitter.... "I am but just arrived.--You hold out bravely against a superior force...."

"We had just got the upper hand, when this Pappenheim came up with his cuirassiers, and made the issue of the fight again doubtful.... Do you see him there with raised visor on a grey horse how he is animating his troopers? he seems to stamp on the ground and call up ever fresh masses of death-defying cuirassiers--but forward, friend!"

Gabriel on his black horse pressed irresistibly forward. The troop of horsemen, that followed his waving plume, advanced deepest into the fray. His gigantic form, overtopping all about him, and the unwearied strength of his arm, that scattered his enemies like stubble, attracted Pappenheim's attention. He had hitherto encouraged his Walloons by the brandishing of his glittering sabre, and the thunder of his voice, that was perfectly audible over the roar of battle; but at sight of the bold onward movement of this enemy's officer he suddenly resolved, like a Grecian hero of antiquity, once more to assay the oft-proved might of his sword. His afterwards world-renowned youthful rashness carried him where the throng was densest, and Mannsfield's out-lawed General was soon confronted by Count

Pappenheim, the most zealous servant of his Emperor, the most ardent champion of his faith.--Both men were of gigantic stature, both felt, that by one well-aimed stroke a loss might be inflicted on the opposite party which would with difficulty be repaired. Gabriel heeded not his fixed intention, nor Pappenheim the duty of a leader; forgetful of every other consideration it seemed as if each of them desired but to achieve the object immediately before him or die.--A life and death combat ensued between the two officers, a combat such as most rarely occurs in modern warfare. Each gazed for a second motionlessly in the other's face. Pappenheim observed with astonishment a bright streak of purple, like a sacrificial flame, on the forehead of his antagonist, while Gabriel stared at the crossed swords on Pappenheim's brow.--That was the Pappenheim, that was the mark, of which the student, nine days ago at the dinner-table of his landlord, Reb Schlome Sachs' had spoken, the same student who had reminded him of his father and mother.--All the past, the immediate future, passed with the infinite-swiftness of thought before his mental vision. He desired to live, to live for his revenge. The mournful presentiment, that to-day, so near the longed for goal, he must die without having attained it, the mournful presentiment, with which he had once before on this day been imbued, sprung up with redoubled violence in his breast. That an adverse destiny should have led him to-day, this very day, against the doughtiest champion of the Imperial army!... He would gladly have retreated, but again he had gone too far, it was no longer possible to withdraw. Pappenheim stormed against him with all the mad audacity of youthful ardour, a terrible combat began. Both were unusually powerful men, both were accomplished swordsmen. Pappenheim had expected to encounter an opponent skilful as himself, but he found his master. The foreboding of death which had passed over Gabriel, had not dispirited but had made him cautious, he had acted for some time on a system of defence, but suddenly spied a weak point in his adversary's too impetuous attack and, raising himself suddenly in saddle, planted a masterly thrust which his knightly foe could not parry with sufficient rapidity.... Pappenheim dropped lifeless from his horse.... Gabriel drew a deep breath, and the Bohemian cavalry pressed bravely forward, while the cuirassiers discouraged by the presumed death of their leader began to give ground. Suddenly, however, a rumour flies through the ranks. That young Anhalt has been thrown from his horse wounded, and has fallen into the hands of the Imperialists. Gabriel heard it, and shortly afterwards orders ring out in Bubna's sonorous voice, who had succeeded to the command in place of young Anhalt--Still there is hope of victory: but the whole aspect of affairs is speedily changed.

Simultaneously with the attack upon the Bohemian right wing the Duke upon his own right had made a feigned false attack of Poles and Cossacks against the Hungarian cavalry drawn up opposite to them, an attack however soon repelled and dissipated by the resistance it encountered. The Hungarians, whose chief Bornemissa was unable to sit on horseback, allowed themselves to be deceived by this stratagem; they pursued the fugitives and looking upon themselves as already masters of the field, broke their serried ranks to seek for plunder. Duke Maximilian and Lichtenstein, who had been watching for this favourable moment, advanced with fresh choice troops against the Hungarians. Anhalt saw the danger that threatened his left, and sent reinforcements from Hohenlohe's cavalry in the centre to the aid of the hard-pressed troops. But Lichtenstein received them with a well-directed fire of cannon and musketry, the front ranks fell, and Hohenlohe's cavalry took to sudden flight without having struck a blow. A panic terror seized the Hungarians, they followed the bad example that had been given them, turned their backs upon the enemy and burst through the ranks of their own infantry. Every effort to stop the flight of the Hungarians, was vain, they threw themselves into the valley near Motol, and endeavoured to cross the Moldau by swimming; but the river was swollen, and most of them found their grave under its waves. The infantry, thrown into disorder, deserted by the cavalry and without artillery, was itself also now obliged to make up its mind for a speedy retreat.--The left wing and centre of the Bohemian army was beaten, Lichtenstein and Boucquoi had no longer an enemy before them. The Duke also made a sweep round with his right wing and main-body to the left and occupied the heights, on which Anhalt had planted the whole of his artillery, and from which his troops had advanced too far. In a short time it was in the hands of the Duke, and Frederick's soldiers were exposed to the fire of their own cannon. This happened exactly at the moment when Pappenheim had fallen, Anhalt had been taken prisoner by the Imperialists and Bubna had succeeded to the command.--Bubna ordered a retreat to be sounded. The troops, in rear exposed to the fire of the artillery, in front to the terrible onset of the Imperial cavalry, now as their services were no longer needed elsewhere united in one body,--retired in as good order as the unfavourable circumstances would admit of.--A bit of high ground to which they had fought their way between two fires revealed to them the comfortless aspect of the field of battle.... Corpses and arms that had been cast away strewed the plain. The centre and left wing was discovered in full flight. A determination had to be quickly taken. It was necessary to separate. Bubna decided that he would endeavour to conduct the horse back to Prague, so as at least to preserve the remnant of his cavalry for Frederick. Schlick and his Moravian infantry is firmly resolved to die rather than fly, and while Bubna accompanied by Gabriel turns in the direction of Prague, the Moravian regiments in serried ranks press through the victorious Imperial army, and fighting their way reach the wood of Stern, where they again make a stand, but soon succumb valiantly resisting to the last....

The victory of the Imperialists was complete, and achieved in less than an hour.--Four thousand Bohemians, among them one Count and several noblemen, had fallen. Young Anhalt, young Schlick and other superior officers were prisoners, all the artillery and camp had fallen into the enemy's hands. The loss of the Imperial-Bavarian army had been proportionally small. Count Meggau, Rechberg, and fourteen other officers had remained dead on the field, Godfrey of Pappenheim was afterwards found, alive but badly wounded, under a heap of slain.

Considering the complete overthrow of the Bohemian army, the Duke had held all pursuit of the fugitives unnecessary, and close to Prague, on the highroad, several battalions of infantry that Schlemmersdorf was leading back to Prague united themselves to Bubna's orderly masses of horse.--Schlemmersdorf held out his hand sadly to Bubna and Gabriel: all three rode in silence through the Strahower Gate. As they entered the city they saw the Palatine. He was clad, as for a feast, in satin. Habernfield had not succeeded in persuading him to come to the battle-field, he would not ride out fasting, had purposed that very day to give an entertainment, and would not betake himself to camp till the cloth was drawn. Tidings of the complete overthrow of his troops interrupted the ill-timed banquet, he hurried to the gates, where his Generals, Prince Anhalt and Count Hohenlohe were already coming to meet him. The first was without a helmet and terribly excited.

"Gracious Sire. You have lost the battle, and I my only son on the field!" he cried to him with the agitated grief of an inconsolable father: "all is lost!"

Frederick was for a moment unable to answer, violent emotion deprived him of the power of speech.--"I now know what I am," he said at length, "there are virtues which only misfortune can teach us, and we Princes discover in adversity alone, what manner of men we are."

"Gracious Sire!" now said Schlemmersdorf, who at that moment rode through the gate, in a tone of mournful reproach. "You were sitting joyously and cheerfully at table, while your army let itself be shot down before the gates in your cause."

"And you have made a fruitless sacrifice of yourselves," said Frederick sorrowfully, and a tear filled his eyes: "I am undone!"

"God forbid," cried Schlemmersdorf; "we are bringing the remnant of the army about seventeen battalions to you; the fugitives at the first blast of the trumpet will return to their standards, Mannsfield's flying division stands ready for battle in rear of the enemy, eight thousand fresh troops in support have arrived from Hungary and have already reached Brandeis.... Only give orders for the gates to be shut, and for the burghers to arm and the city can hold out against a long siege."

"What do *you* think, Prince?" Frederick turned to Anhalt. He shrugged his shoulders. "Advise me, gentlemen, advise me, what is your opinion?" cried Frederick almost imploringly, "what should be done?"

"First of all," observed Bubna with a side glance at Anhalt, "a brave general must be nominated to conduct the defence of the city...."

"You have requested my advice, gracious Sire!" Anhalt now continued, "well then, the open street is a bad place for a serious consultation: permit me to accompany you to the castle, there we will think the matter over...."

The battle lost had not diminished Anhalt's influence over the feeble Frederick. The Palatine turned his horse, and accompanied by Anhalt, Hohenlohe and Schlemmersdorf, rode to the Hradschin. Bubna looked after them in bitter wrath.

"What do you think of doing, Bitter?" enquired Bubna after a long and painful pause.

"At all events I shall remain to-night in the city," replied Gabriel, "to-morrow we shall hear, what sort of a plan Frederick's council has hatched, and I shall guide myself accordingly.... It is settled that our Mannsfield shall continue the war, even if Frederick concludes a peace. Whatever happens, I intend to share Mannsfield's fate."

"You are no Bohemian, Bitter! you are free.... but I, I, ... I love not Frederick, I esteem him not:--but the diet has elected him: if he is obliged to leave Prague a fugitive, I must go with him, I cannot act otherwise. Only when he has obtained a secure retreat, shall I join Mannsfield--therefore Bitter, farewell!"

Gabriel pressed Bubna's hand, but suddenly the old soldier threw his arms passionately round Gabriel's neck and kissed him repeatedly with impetuosity. "You saved my life at the skirmish of Netolitz," he said, "I have never thanked you for doing it. I always believed that I should some day repay the old debt. But our paths divide--Bitter! we are approaching a period, insecure, and prolific of disorder: ... The immediate future may bring death to us, I do not know whether we shall ever meet again. Bitter! I feel as if I shall never see thee more.... I thank thee.... farewell!"

Bubna tore himself away by a violent effort, his rough powerful voice shook, large tears flowed slowly over his powder-blackened face. Without leaving Gabriel time to reply, he spurred off in the direction of the Hradschin. But once more he halted and making a signal with his hand, cried, "farewell, Bitter, for ever!"

Gabriel could make no answer from emotion, and was obliged almost to cling to his horse's neck to prevent rocking in his seat.--That strange flutter within him of a sad presentiment of death, when Schlemmersdorf called him to the field, had disappeared in the heat of the fight, but was again powerfully excited when he had stood in single combat against the awful Pappenheim. For a moment he had given himself up as lost beyond redemption. But he had conquered, he had returned without a wound, safe and sound to Prague: it seemed to him as though he had risen superior to destiny. A bold violent feeling of self-confidence in his strength attained to its highest pitch, and spite of bitter discontent for the lost battle, he still smiled within himself at the childish terrors to which he had given way. But Bubna's leave-taking, the gloomy presentiment, which the aged, gallant veteran steeled in many a battle had undoubtedly given voice to, and which Gabriel had involuntarily referred to himself, had once again violently shaken him. In swift course, as though to leave his gloomy thoughts behind, he spurred over the bridge into the Altstadt, and first held rein in the Marienplatz before his residence. His devoted armourer was waiting for him impatiently at the gate.

"Thank God, gracious Sir, you live; you are not wounded.... The battle is lost, is it not?"

Gabriel hurried, without heeding the armourer's words up the steps and beckoned him to follow. Gabriel threw himself into an arm chair, the armourer stood straight as a taper before him, expecting his orders.

"Martin!" began the General after a long reflection; "you have always been faithful to me, from my heart I thank you for it--you must do me one more service, perhaps the last. This night will decide the fate of Prague, of the whole country. I do not doubt that Frederick will follow the whispered suggestions of his council, will fly; ... in that case the ensuing morning must not find me in Prague.... I dare not fall alive into the hands of the Imperialists...."

"Only, gracious Sir, fly," interposed Martin, rubbing the back of his hand across his moist eyes; "don't lose a moment!"

"No, Martin! I must stay here to-night, I *must* Martin!" he repeated impetuously, as if the man had contradicted him; then rapidly paced the chamber, and said softly to himself. "How, if Frederick were cowardly and wicked enough to open at once and instantly the gates of Prague for the entrance of the enemy.--How if I, the outlaw, should fall alive into the hands of the Imperialists, if I, born in ignominy, should die ignominiously by the hand of the executioner, should die without having avenged myself; ... No, no, I stay in Prague at all hazards, I *must* revenge myself.... and then?... surely I have a trusty sword, I will never fall alive into the hands of my enemy.... Martin!" he said aloud, "in every event let two of the dragoons who accompanied me to Prague, wait for me to-morrow morning early at the Schweinthor well armed and with a saddled horse. If in the course of the night the city is put into a state of defence, it will be announced to the burghers and you will hear of it. If this is not the case, we must conclude that Frederick gives up all idea of resistance, surrenders his crown.--The best plan will be for you to go to the Hradschin and watch carefully whether the Palatine takes flight. No carriage can pass out of the city unperceived. To-morrow at daybreak you come to the gate and make your report to me. If the city is given up, I shall go to Brandeis to meet the Hungarian reinforcements, endeavour to form a junction between them and Mannsfield, and the war begins anew.--If the Imperialists march in, they will seek me; say that I escaped with the Palatine."

"Gracious Sir!" cried Martin, "fly at once, tarry not a moment. I will fly with you, I will never forsake you."

"What is the matter with you?" said Gabriel, moved in spite of the disorder of his spirits by the armourer's proposal. "You are now a domiciled citizen of Prague, no one will trouble himself about you, and when the first storm, which will only touch lofty heads, has blown itself out, you can go on with your business in peace. Consider, old man! you have only one leg, you are no longer young, a soldier's life is no longer suitable for you.... or are you afraid lest they should pay you out for your fidelity to me? No, Martin! there is no fear of that, they do not know of it, and even if they did know!..."

"No, it is not that, gracious Sir," replied Martin; "I only fear on your account. Why will you pass this night in Prague?... fly at once!"

"I *cannot*, Martin! I *cannot*," said Gabriel; "it will be time enough to fly to-morrow.... I adhere to the directions that I have given. Now leave me alone, I have still matters to think over.--We shall see one another to-morrow."

Martin lingered yet another moment. "Gracious Sir!" he said.

"Do you still wish to say anything?... Yes, I recollect, I must reward you for your faithful service, and to-morrow in my hurry I might forget it ..." Gabriel began to unlock a cabinet.

"For God's sake. Sir! How could you misunderstand me so? that is not what I desire, I am rich enough:--but grant me this favour--fly to-day, fly at once...."

Martin's obstinacy was striking. "What reason have you? Have you any information? Do you think that a rising in favour of the Imperialists will break out in the city? speak!

"No, by God Almighty, I have no information, gracious Sir!... but," he added in a low unsteady voice, "I fear, I know not why, that I shall never see you alive again to-morrow."

Gabriel gave an involuntary shudder. The words of the honest armourer accorded so exactly with Bubna's farewell.--

"Martin!" he said, after he had recovered his self-possession, "your love to me makes you take a gloomy view of everything.... I cannot set off today, I *must stay here*--my resolution is immovable!"

Martin bowed himself over the hand, which Gabriel extended to him, and wetted it with his tears.

"My resolve is unshakeable!" repeated Gabriel once more when he was alone.... this was the last word that he had addressed to Blume.... He paced the room with long strides. Physical exhaustion, unusual but easily to be accounted for, increased his intense mental excitement. His stirring life had been always full of manifold vicissitudes, but to-day in the short space of a few hours an infinity of events had been compressed. Once awakened and kept alive by suggestion, from many quarters, he could not quite banish from his soul the thought that he should die *to-day this very day*. He had often been near to death, the enemies' balls had often whistled about him, hostile daggers had threatened him, he might often before have fallen, and unavenged, and without having accomplished his design:--*But he had never been so near it*--on the faintest doubt of the success of his plan he suffered the tortures, which legend attributes to Tantalus: only more woeful.... *If he should die to-day without having revenged himself, if he should die, behind him a desolate, empty, aimless existence, before him an unknown future, then there must be a Providence, then he must have ruined more than one human life, more than one existence.*--He struggled with the whole strength of his powerful intellect against the thought that would keep rising from the depths of his soul. But the thought was intangible, irrefutable. He might assure himself thousands of times, that there was no ground for these terrors, but for the very reason that he found no sensible foundation for his apprehensions, this inexplicable coincidence of his own sensations with that of his friend Bubna, of his devoted Martin, caused him a feeling of uneasy astonishment.--But his strong mind gradually with many a struggle composed itself. He could not in truth annihilate the painful thought, but he overcame it.

"Blume's fate, her husband's life is still in my hands," he said to himself. "The immediate future may cause an alteration in our relative positions.... the grey dawn of to-morrow must not find me in Prague.... I do not know whether I shall ever see Blume again--the favourable moment for revenge must be made use of!"

One hour later Gabriel was about to step out of the back-door of his house. He was again in the dress of a student, but he had this time thrown a broad cloak about him.

"What do you want, Martin?" he enquired in surprise, as he saw the armourer, who caught him hurriedly by the arm.

"Sir," cried he, "do not enter the Jews' quarter, fly, quit the silly passion.... he entreated; what signify Jewish women to you?... do not go into the Jews' town, they are well affected to the Emperor there."

"Martin! you mean well ... but I cannot follow your advice--See," he unfolded his cloak, under which flashed a scabbard and three pistols, "I am armed, there is nothing to be afraid of. Leave me, you know me, you are aware that my resolution is immovable.--Remember, to-morrow early at the Schweinsthor."

Gabriel stepped out and hastened to the Jews' street. Martin gazed after him as long as he was in sight, then closed the postern and murmured with a sigh: "surely I shall never see him again."

The news of Fredericks complete overthrow had soon spread over the whole city, and the highest excitement prevailed everywhere. The burghers of the Altstadt had sent up to the castle, to ask what they should do, and offered themselves to enlist troops and defend the city if Frederick would remain in Prague. Frederick's answer, which he communicated to the burghers by Anhalt's advice: "that they should endeavour to make terms with the enemy, for himself he would depart at daybreak" was not as yet known. The inhabitants of the Altstadt, well disposed to Frederick, were overwhelmed, the population of the Kleinseite on the other hand, being for the most part devoted to the Emperor, rejoiced at the victory which Duke Maximilian had won. Great excitement too prevailed in the Jews' town. Numerous groups in the open street were whispering the latest intelligence; all were of the Imperial faction. Gabriel hurried through this throng. At the corner of a street he happened to run against a crowd of students. He recognised them, they were in the habit of attending the lecture room of the

Assessor Reb Lippmann Heller, the same which Gabriel, in order to keep up at least the outward appearance of a student, had attended.

"How do you do Reb Gabriel;" one of the students turned quickly round, "How do you do? a pity you were not at lecture this morning, it was a lecture! I tell you, you can only hear one like it in Prague--wonderful!"

The student who had addressed Gabriel was a strange figure.--He was the Nestor of the Prague students.--He had numbered fifty years. Devoted to the continual study of the Talmud he had found it best after a mature deliberation of five and twenty years to renounce all ideas of marriage. In early days these may very well have been wrecked upon his outward appearance, which in fact offered little that was attractive. His unusual height did not in the remotest degree harmonise with a remarkable leanness that served as a foil to an enormous humped back. His dress was moreover calculated to intensify the strange impression produced by his appearance. Of a poor family, and too devoted to study to earn a living by teaching, he was perpetually driven to make use of his friends' cast off clothes. This he did without paying the least attention to their physical stature, and so it came to pass, that his threadbare silken doublet scarce covered his hump, that the much-darned slovenly cloth-breeches turned up their ends at the knee, where they should by right have joined on to the somewhat ragged silk stockings and left a notable gap very imperfectly filled up by a linen band; that the little close fitting cap, whose original black tended towards a very significant red, rested but lightly on his head covered with thick masses of hair, and shook about at the slightest movement of the vivacious man. A grey beard, that hung untended down on his breast, was continually combed out by the fingers of his right hand, and when its bearer was engaged in any animated discussion was forced to submit to have its end turned up artistically into his mouth, and to be bitten, and in fact Reb Mordechai Wag's--that was the student's name--teeth had manifestly thinned this ornamental hair appendage. Notwithstanding this very unattractive exterior, Reb Mordechai Wag was everywhere well received. He had a quick intelligence that readily grasped the essence of Talmud truth, and a good heart. On account of his dialectics, he was a terror to all itinerant teachers who wished to lecture in Prague and a patron of all the humble students who came to the high school there. Often, when as was the custom at that time, he was invited by some member of the community to dinner, he sent some one else in his place, who, less fortunate than himself had found no host that day, and while he gave out that he was ill, chewed his small crust of dry bread at home, and laughed at his own cunning. Study of the Talmud was the one highest aim of his life. It seemed to him impossible that a student could take interest in anything besides a lecture, and even to-day, when everything was in the greatest uproar, it was perfectly indifferent to him, whether the Palatine or the Duke Maximilian gained the victory, and his thoughts ran only in their accustomed track.--It was very unpleasant for Gabriel, just in his present temper, to have fallen into the hands of the sympathetic Reb Mordechai, and yet he was unwilling to draw the attention of the students to himself by making off in too great a hurry. He enveloped himself therefore more closely in the cloak that concealed his arms, and said struggling with his impatience: "I am sorry to have missed to-day's lecture, I shall take the earliest opportunity of asking you to impart to me what the...."

"Why put it of? I will tell you at once: what have we got better to do now?"

"I thought," replied Gabriel forcing a laugh, "a moment when every one looks excitedly forward to see what will happen next, when it will be decided whether the Emperor or the Palatine...."

"What does that matter to us students?" interrupted Reb Mordechai, provoked by Gabriel's opposition.... "The Emperor will be a mild ruler.... the Palatine and the Bohemian nobility have also protected us Jews, but how can that be helped, they haven risen against the government, and you know, that is not right.--But let us leave all that to the Holy one, praised be his name--and occupy ourselves with an exposition of his words.... the master then...."

"Reb Mordechai," now interposed a young man with a dark expressive countenance, whom the others called Reb Michoel; "leave that for the present. It is a fine thing when learning is combined with knowledge of the world.... The affairs of this world are also of importance even though you cannot understand it; you come from outside," he continued turning to Gabriel, "have you perchance heard anything more authentic about the battle? It is reported, that the Hungarian cavalry was at first victorious, but that the heavy artillery of the Imperialists had silenced the fire of the small...."

"What does it signify to a student," asked Reb Mordechai vehemently, "whether the cavalry fired on the infantry, or the infantry on the cavalry, whether they first let off the small firelocks and then the great guns, or contrariwise? What rightly constituted student troubles him about such things? A student may become a Rabbi, or a butcher, or peaceful father of a family, but have you ever seen a student that became a soldier?"

A third youth who had as yet taken no share in the conversation drew nearer. "I have only been a short time in Prague," he said, "I have up to this time been studying at Frankfurt on Main, I am not aware whether the name of Gabriel Süss is known to you.... he was first an able student, and then became a soldier."

Gabriel shrunk within himself; he heard himself thus named for the first time since many years, he made no answer, but Michoel shook his head negatively. "Gabriel Süss.... Süss"--repeated Reb Mordechai thoughtfully, "was not he a bastard? I once heard something about it.... but I have no memory for such trifling matters."

"What happened to him?" asked Michoel inquisitively, "tell us, I pray you."

Reb Nochum--that was the name of the Frankfurt student--complied with Reb Michoel's urgent request, and related Gabriel's history, departing indeed here and there somewhat from the truth, but on the whole correctly enough. His story concluded thus, that Gabriel had once since his baptism been seen by early acquaintances on horseback with several Imperial troopers, but might perhaps, as he had disappeared since that time, have met his death in the Juliers and Cleves war.

"Yes, I have heard something of the kind," said Mordechai, when the Frankfurt student had finished; "but it was not known in Prague that he had become a soldier, it was reported that he had drowned himself; who knows however whether it was true.... Besides you know, he might have been declared legitimate, yes truly," added Mordechai hastily, feeling himself once more on firm ground, "The mothers declaration is worth nothing, Gabriel Süss ought not to be looked upon as a bastard, refer to the Jad-ha-Chasaka cap. 15 &c." ...

"That's all very well, Reb Mordechai," replied Michoel, "but you forget, it was a dying mother, a dying mother will not part from her child with a lie.... and moreover she had ever till then, as this story is told, loved her son.... besides, what would be the use to him? Will any one, will any one person doubt, that he is a bastard? If you had a sister or daughter, would you give her to him to wife? think of that, Reb Mordechai: *No power on earth could establish the legality of his birth before our inward convictions!*"

Michoel's glance chanced to rest upon Gabriel's face, he noticed the fiery red, and deadly pallor that coursed in quick succession over Gabriel's features.--"*Not before inward conviction,*" echoed Gabriel, feebly.--Reb Mordechai had no answer to make, and a pause ensued. Gabriel might now have got away, but he would not, the conversation was too interesting to him not to hear the end of it.

"The law: that a bastard may not enter into the congregation of the Lord," began Reb Nochum again, "is unreasonable. Why should the innocent be punished for the sins of his parents? Why is he cast forth from the closest, loveliest union? Why may he never lead home a loving woman as wife? Why may he not be happy in the circle of his family? Yet consider, even in this law the spirit of the Lord comes to light, which breathes upon the faithful out of every word of Holy Scripture. Contemplate this bastard, this Gabriel Süss.... he cursed his inanimate mother: ... only a bastard could do that, no man could perpetrate such an iniquity, unless he were born in sin.... The transgression, that called him into life, urges him ever farther forward, and involuntarily he trod the paths of sin.... therefore the Lord in his wisdom may...."

"You are a thinker," Michoel interrupted the speaker, "and I am glad to have met you: such are not often found among students.... *A firm faith in God is not shaken by reasonable speculations, if they are kept properly subordinate.* But you are in error friend! God forbid, that any man should be obliged to follow a path absolutely fixed beforehand, the path of sin.--Where would his free will be? that is not so. You may not give a daughter or sister to a bastard as wife, so the commentaries enjoin us--but only that and nothing further is declared by the Talmud--that is a command, like many others, a command of the Lord's, obscure and inexplicable to man's mind.... but a bastard may be noble, great, a shining light to his people. Are you not acquainted with the article 'a bastard profoundly versed in scripture is superior in dignity to a high priest who is less deserving.' Is it not true," Michoel turned to Mordechai, "that it is so. Gabriel Süss ought not to have despaired, ought not to have acted as he did. The Lord had blessed him with earthly wealth, had endued him with a powerful intellect: he might have been a benefactor of the poor, a staff to the infirm, a teacher of his people, an example of humble submission. In the enjoyment of the highest mental activity, the undisturbed study of God's word, in strivings for a future state, he might have found consolation, and peace even in this world. *His fate was in his own hands.... it was his own fault that he perished.*"

Gabriel felt as if a blazing thunderbolt had fallen in the depths of his soul. He pressed his hands spasmodically against his heart and was forced to sit down upon the curb-stone. Mordechai, whose understanding was not transcendent enough to appreciate the force of what had just been said, observed this as little as Reb Nochum, whose attention remained entirely fixed upon Michoel's words. It was only the sharp glance of this latter that noticed Gabriel's emotion, which he was incapable of controlling.--*The state of frightful excitement,* of feverish expectation in which he found himself, *had still more intensified and exaggerated the impression of those words.* He felt at this moment with the whole power of his comprehension that in the most decisive events of his life the torch of his wild hatred had been his only light, that everything had come grinning to meet him distorted by its gloomy dismal rays.... The words which might once have fallen like assuaging balsam upon his bleeding heart now struck him with the whole weight of their convincing truth. The thought, that might once have saved him, now filled him with nameless unutterable woe. The audacious confidence with which he had believed himself irresponsible for all that he had done was broken--Michoel had shown him what he might have been--how different had he become!

A pause had again ensued. Mordechai now observed with horror that he was almost too late for evening-prayer, and hurried with Reb Nochum into the nearest synagogue. Michoel remained standing before Gabriel who seemed nearly to have lost consciousness. At last he asked, recovering himself, in a dull voice: "Who are you and what is your name?"

"I am Michoel Glogau, I was born in Silesia, and have finished here my course of Talmudic study. I have been summoned to Breslau as preacher--and what is your name?"

"I am called Gabriel Mar," he replied to the interrogation in a trembling unsteady voice.

"Gabriel Mar, Mar, Mar," echoed Michoel quite softly and thoughtfully, his eyes fast fixed on Gabriel: "strange!... are you unwell, that you sit there thus languidly on the stones?"

"Yes.... no.... rather--I shall soon be better. Why do you gaze at me so fixedly? only go away, Reb Michoel, do not be disturbed on my account.... I am often wont.... to suffer so. Away, I pray you, away, away...."

Michoel went off, stopping from time to time to look round after Gabriel. He sat for some minutes as if changed to stone, but--whether it was recovered self-possession, or whether the heavy snow which began to fall had roused him--he got up suddenly, wiped the cold sweat from his forehead and looked motionlessly at the spot where Michoel had stood, as if to convince himself, that they were not fantastic dreams which hovered over him, then hurriedly strode to his dwelling. As he arrived at the end of the narrow lane that led out of the Jews-town to the Old-synagogue, he suddenly heard his old name Gabriel Süss called. Taken by surprise he involuntarily turned his head--he saw no one and hastened with redoubled speed to his house by the Old-synagogue.

"It is he!" said Michoel stepping from behind the corner of a wall that had concealed him from Gabriel's sight, "my suspicion was correct, Gabriel Mar--is Gabriel Süss. I must speak with him."

Gabriel was once more in his room by the Old-synagogue. In a few hours, since the forenoon when Schlemmersdorf had summoned him to the battle-field, what numberless events had happened within and without him. Frederick had lost his crown, the Emperor had won a highly important victory. He had been present at this weighty catastrophe, had been a witness, a participator in the hot combat, his life had been threatened on all sides. He had stood opposed to Pappenheim, the most accomplished knight in the Imperial army, and believed that he had slain him--and all these occurrences of which any one would have been sufficient to have put the most strong minded into a state of intensest excitement disappeared and left no trace in Gabriel's soul. Michoel's words had called forth a fresh flood of emotion in his overcharged breast. A new sorrow never before anticipated strove with the old grief in his breast. With the whole gigantic strength of his intellect he endeavoured to swing himself up out of the wild chaos of thoughts which would have indubitably thrown any one of weaker mould into the black night of madness.--With both his mighty hands pressed against his inflamed and glowing lofty brow, as if to force all thoughts to one point, he sat for hours by the table in strong inward struggle.

"No, no, no!" he cried out at length impetuously, "now it is too late, too late! Gabriel, thou hast gone, too far, too far, now thou canst never recede.--Thou art like that Acher, he that heard said of himself: 'Turn again ye stiffnecked children.... all but Acher!'--Yes Michoel. Thou man with a beautiful voice, with mild friendly gleaming eyes! Hadst thou stood at my mother's death-bed, hadst thou then addressed me thus.... but they had all rejected me.... Oh, Blume! Blume! Why did you treat me so? Had you but extended to me, *I will not say your hand, but your compassion*.... Alas! one single word of comfort on that day of atonement, in my fierce wrestling with the unutterable grief! Why did you not speak like this Michoel? Oh! I should have been quite another man, surely, surely, I should have been a changed man!... Blume! you might have been the preserving angel of my life.... You cast me from you, you became my demon!... Gabriel held both hands before his face: yes, *you, you*," he now suddenly cried, and wild fury repressed all gentle feelings, "*you* have forced me to take the path which I tread.... you have poisoned my existence, annihilated my hopes!... If I now stand between a comfortless past and a hopeless future, I will at least turn the present to account, I will at least bring my ruined wretched life to a consistent conclusion. I will avenge myself, sweetly, fearfully.... This night I dedicate to revenge--and then--myself to certain death: the next battle I will hurl myself where the enemies' ranks are thickest, will bathe my naked breast in a warm shower of bullets. One blade, one ball will surely find its way to my heart broken with sorrow!--and when alone and forsaken, trampled by horses' feet on the bloody plain, I expire: then will I raise my failing eyes for one last defiant look, then with unbending spirit I will once more exclaim: Where art thou whom men call, all just, all mighty, all merciful? Dost thou behold? I die desolate forsaken unwept,--cursed by the woman whom once I madly loved, rejected by the father...."

This thought, that had been woven like a red thread through Gabriel's spiritual life, this thought, that had continually buoyed him with hope or racked him with despair, according as the waves of his troubled spirit were rising or falling, now worked upon Gabriel, only if possible more violently, if possible, with greater tenacity. He tore open the window in almost mad haste, and looked up to the partially clouded starry heaven: "Give me my father, if thou art Almighty, let me find him, find him *to-day, to-day*.... and I will offer up to thee the greatest sacrifice, the woefullest sacrifice, the sacrifice of my revenge; let me die in my father's arms ..., and I will perform my vow, yes, yes, I will bow my stiff neck as I die, *I will repent, will say that I have sinned, that thou art all merciful, all just, Almighty!* my last breath shall be a 'Hear o Israel'.--I will die like a pious Jew: but thou must give me my father, give him *to-day*! Canst thou do that. Almighty one?"

The phrensied scornful laughter with which he accompanied these last words, echoed over the empty court, and reverberated dull and hollow from the spacious adjacent vaults of the opposite synagogue, the lofty windows of which chanced to be open.

In the highest state of bodily and mental tension Gabriel sank back in his chair, the warm stream of blood that had rushed to his head and threatened to burst his forehead, flowed again slowly back to his heart: a sudden collapse, as is often the case, followed after this indescribable excitement; after this, but later, a calm reflective mood. In this state his landlady Schöndel found him, when she opened the door, and asked: "Reb Gabriel, you are sitting in the dark, do you wish for candles?"

Accepting Gabriel's silence as consent, she disappeared directly to fetch a light.

On his return home Gabriel had laid his weapons upon the table; he wished to hide them quickly before Schöndel returned with a light. A large old bureau, belonging to his landlord, stood near him: but the key was not in the lock. Without stopping to reflect he opened its bottom drawer with a strong kick and threw the arms into it. A moment afterwards Schöndel entered with a light: Gabriel leaned heavily against the broken bureau to conceal it from Schöndel.

"Where have you been all day, Reb Gabriel?" she asked, "we have not seen you since early morning! What do you say to the news of to-day?... We in the Jews-town are absolutely without information; perhaps by to-morrow morning early the Imperialists will already occupy the circle of the Altstadt."

"Indeed, then I must make haste," said Gabriel.

"Why make haste?" enquired Schöndel with an air of surprise.

"That is quite clear," answered Gabriel recovering himself, with a forced laugh. "I have now been rather a long time in Prague and have to speak the truth not studied much Talmud. I must recommence. If the city is surrendered, everybody's attention will be diverted, I myself shall be disturbed, and my good intentions will be again postponed for some days. I will set to work this very day. At midnight I shall go to the lecture room and study all night long. Then before daybreak I shall go to prayers in the Old-synagogue. I suppose the gate will be open early enough?"

"Yes, but you must be in the Jews-town two hours before midnight or the gates will be shut ... Well, I am heartily rejoiced that you intend beginning to behave like a real student.... but you will not come to prayers to-morrow morning, I give you my word of that?"

"Why not?" asked Gabriel.

"Early to-morrow you will be sleeping a deep sleep, out of which a person does not easily awaken."--Schöndel heard her husband's voice calling her and hurried away. Gabriel had misunderstood the last words. Students, who staid awake the whole night in a lecture-room, were in the habit of falling asleep towards morning and so being late for early service. This was what Schöndel had meant jokingly to signify: but Gabriel was in no mood to understand a joke, and these words sounded gloomily and bodingly.... they accorded so strangely with the terror of the faithful armourer, with Bubna's affecting farewell, with the mournful presentiment that had many times in the course of the day taken possession of him!

The stroke of the clock on the Rathhaus indicated that hour which corresponds to eight in the evening. He wished to be in the Jews-town before the gates were shut, two hours before midnight, so that he had still some time before him. The superhuman excitement of the day, the delicious torment of the expectation of revenge, that kept all his manly energy on the stretch, could not long continue in such strength. He was afraid, that the excess of these sensations would drive him mad, would kill him. He passed his strong hand over his lofty brow, and firmly closed his eyes, as though to annihilate thought.... He sought for some object adapted to occupy his mind otherwise for two hours:--one suddenly offered itself to him. A manuscript had fallen out of the bureau when it was violently broken open.--He now noticed this for the first time. He picked up the sealed packet, it was written in Hebrew, and the envelope informed him, that it was the history, the testament of Reb Mosche, his landlady's father, which was to be first opened twenty years after his death. He locked the door of his room, pushed the chair to the table: unsealed the writings and read.--Its contents were as follows:

"On the 23d day of the month Tischri, that is the day which succeeds the feast of tents, in the year 371 according to the lesser Jewish reckoning. It will be seven and thirty years to-day since I kept my 13th birthday, and now I have reached my 50th year. On the same day too I left the ancient, worthy community of Prague--in which I had passed my youth, and where God willing, I will end my days--on a wide and weary wandering."

"I cannot employ this day more holily than by beginning to write the leaves of my biography; the leaves which I intend for you my children. When you break the seal of these writings I shall have been for years no longer among the living; but as a father's infinite love reaches far beyond the grave, so will your recollection of me survive, and you will not then refuse me the fullest sympathy.--I have written down the narrative of my life, that at least after my death there may be no mystery between us.

"My father, may the memory of the just be blessed, was that most learned Talmudist and Cabbalist Rabbi Jizchok Meduro. He was descended from a very old family that flourished for centuries in Spain, and his ancestors had always made themselves conspicuous from learning and attachment to their faith.--Fearful and bloody persecutions of the Jews had compelled his father, a little orphan boy, to a formal change of faith. When arrived at man's estate it repented him that he had, though but in outward profession, laid aside the faith of his father's, and when the officers of the inquisition discovered him at a celebration of the Passover, and led him before the tribunal, he openly confessed that with all his soul he was a Jew. He mounted the scaffold at Seville. He sang psalms and hymns with devout mind, while the flames with a thousand greedy tongues licked up his bloody body, at length a jet of flame shot up into his face and extinguished the light of his eyes. One 'Hear oh Israel' escaped in a suffocated voice from the breast of the dying man--at the same moment a heart-rending cry, a cry that made the bones creep, resounded from the Cathedral square, and a woman fell down lifeless. It was the wife of the dying man; she was pregnant with my father. Two hours afterwards he saw the light of this world in a dismal cellar--

soon after her delivery, his mother succumbed to the most maddening grief. The day of my father's birth was the day of his parents' death. A small red flame was observed on the forehead of the new-born child, an effect of the frightful torture, which the horrible sight of the scaffold had inflicted on the mother stricken with mortal terror.--Devout Jews, themselves in want of every assistance, took care of the helpless orphaned babe, noble mothers suckled him at their breasts. But bigotry was not satisfied with the bloody sacrifice. Another of those frequently recurring persecutions of the Jews had broken out in the Spanish peninsula; there were to be no more Jews in Spain. Whoever would not abjure the old faith was to leave the country within four months without carrying with him silver or gold. A hundred thousand souls forsook goods and possessions to save their relics in a far country, to escape from a land, where their prayer to the one true God was stamped as a crime. A number of noble men, who crossed the sea to Barbary, carried the baby with them, in order to preserve the offspring of so illustrious family for its faith. But the poor people, without money and without protection, were rejected from the coast, a portion of the fugitives succumbed to the plague, a portion fell into the hands of pirates that carried them into captivity: some however were so fortunate as to find a refuge in Portugal after terrible sufferings.--Among these was my father. He had in the meanwhile grown to be a glorious boy. He had as yet experienced nothing but sorrow. The infinite crushing misfortunes that had marked the day of his birth had made an indelible impression on his mind, and even on his features.--A profound abiding melancholy rested on the boy's thoughtful face, and the red fiery spot that sparkled on his forehead never allowed him for a moment to forget that flaming scaffold that had consumed the body of a loved idolised father, the sight of which had caused the death of his mother.

"The youth Jizchock Meduro soon discovered a wisdom almost equal to Solomon's, a fervent love for the faith. He was worthy of his renowned ancestors. Leading a solitary life, he found consolation only in religious studies, and in investigating the powers of nature, and he devoted himself to these pursuits with the greatest zeal. His immense industry, added to unusual intellectual gifts, enabled him to obtain the most beautiful results and the youthful Jizchok Meduro was soon accounted one of the lights of the Portuguese Jewish society.

"My father had attained the age in which he thought it right to choose a wife. His choice fell upon a Spanish orphan, whose father, of firm faith and devout, had also expired upon the scaffold.--In the first year of a happy marriage she gave birth to twins, myself and brother. The small cosy family circle seemed to banish the spirit of melancholy from my father, and not indeed to extinguish but soften his sorrowful recollections. Even this domestic happiness was however soon to be destroyed. Persecutions of the Jews broke out in Portugal also and were soon followed by a royal edict that forced the Jews to change their religion or to leave the country. My father fled with his wife and two children, then in tenderest years. Hunted like wild beasts of the forest, we crossed the Pyrenean peninsula and a part of France. No house, no cottage would hospitably entertain us. At night we were obliged to sleep on the open heath. A drink of water was often refused to the perishing. And we could only attribute it to God's visible protection that after unutterable hardships we reached German ground. In a city on the Rhine our dear mother sunk under the unwonted sufferings of the long journey--she lies buried in Cologne.... My father was alone in a foreign country with two little boys. Too proud even in the misery of exile to be a burden upon his benevolent brethren, he wandered over the whole of Germany, and when at length he arrived in Prague he considered it an interposition of Providence, that the post of upper-servant was vacant in the Old-Synagogue, where the same ritual prevails as in Portugal. He offered himself as a candidate for this office and when he mentioned to the overseer of the synagogue his name the fame of which had reached far into Germany, the latter expressed much regret that my father did not prefer to accept the chair of Rabbi in a community, or whole district. But my father had been too sore afflicted by the strokes of adversity, he desired to live unknown in perfect retirement, for his faith, for his religious studies, for his sons. Nothing could be refused to a man so famous; his wishes were entirely fulfilled by the authorities. Reb Jizchok Meduro became upper-attendant, but it remained a secret to every one else that the servant Reb Jizchok was the great teacher from Portugal. Here then, where I lived as a little boy, and afterwards as man, and where God willing, I will close these wearied eyes, here in this house, which you my dear children now inhabit, lived and studied my deceased father.... His immense knowledge, his wisdom, his ascetic habits, filled every one with a profound reverence for him, which was if possible increased by his kind though reserved manners.

"It was natural that a feeling of reverential respect should also animate myself and brother to the highest degree. Except at prayer we met nobody. Our father never received visits, and as we children did not go to school we had no play-fellows. Our father was all in all to us. In our tender years he had performed for us all the troublesome and petty services of a nurse-maid; as we grew older, he was our instructor; were we sick, he was our physician and nurse.... The profound gravity that rested on his features only gave way to a soft gentle smile when we, my brother and I, sitting below there in the synagogue at his feet, listened to his wonderful expositions, expositions than which since that time I have never heard any so admirable, so inspiriting;

when he perceived how the fire of his mighty eloquence found its way to our youthful hearts and kindled them.--He loved his children infinitely, but refrained from showing it. He never kissed us, once only when he thought that I was asleep, he pressed his lips to my forehead, and a scalding tear rolled down on my face--a sweet rapturous shudder crept over my limbs but I did not venture to open my eyes."

Gabriel stopped at this passage. The image of that pale tall man, who had once pressed his hot lips upon his own young forehead, whose tears had once wetted his face, now appeared vividly, more vividly than ever before him. He now felt sure that this image of his youth had been no dream, and believed himself convinced that if it were now to appear before him he should recognise him, him whom he held to be his father.

Gabriel read on:--

"This proof of his affection encouraged me on that day to the timid question, what was the meaning of the purple streak upon his forehead, a mark, that also at time showed itself on us children when we were violently excited. I had expected a monosyllabic answer from my taciturn father, but contrary to his wont he recounted to us with the whole power of his mournful recollection the terrible events of his life. These we now learnt for the first time, we learnt for the first time, the place of our mother's grave.... 'The spot, that sparkles on my, on your foreheads,' concluded my father, '*is a remembrance of the man from whom we are descended,* who suffered the most painful death in sure trust upon God.... May it be ever remind you to be worthy of your ancestors....'"

Gabriel laid down the manuscript. The fiery mark upon his own forehead now seemed to burn him painfully.... Was he, just at the moment when he desired to come to a violent and complete rupture with his earlier past life, was he, just at the moment when he was giving up all hope of finding his father, that nobler aim of his life, was he just at that very moment to find a direction post? Might not the mark whereby to remember, be also a mark whereby to recognise? After short reflection he once more seized the manuscript with feverish haste and read further:--

"These confidences made an immense impression upon us children, and often, as we sat idly by twilight before the gate of the synagogue, we discussed our father's narrative with mournful emotion, always coming to the conclusion, that we would do all in our power to sweeten our father's life, and some day, when we were grown up, to wander to Cologne to pray at our mother's grave.... I have already mentioned, that we, I and my brother, had no playmates; but in truth we did not care to associate with other children; the infelt brotherly love, with which we were mutually penetrated, quite filled our young minds. Chance, or rather God's providence, guided me however to a young friend, a friend who became the stay of my life.... I had once gone on a commission from my father to an artisan who had some work to deliver for the house of the Lord. My way home led me by the banks of the Moldau. A pack of wild schoolboys were insulting and ill-using a delicate Jewish boy, apparently of about my own age. His cry for help aroused my warmest sympathy. Born under a hot Southern sun, I did not reflect that I was but ten years old and alone, but threw myself into the thick of the throng, and came to the assistance of the poor maltreated child at that moment when two of the worst, irritated by his feeble resistance, would have tossed him into the river. 'Do you want to kill the lad?' I cried with the whole force of my young voice, 'the river is deep, he will be drowned! The first that touches him is a dead man!'

"My arrival, the decided tone of my speech, made the wild troop hesitate for a minute; but immediately afterwards a scornful horse laugh resounded. Naturally strong, indignation gave me double force. With a powerful blow of the fist I compelled the biggest of them, who had got tight hold of the poor sufferer, to let him go. I disengaged the little pale Jew-boy who was bleeding at mouth and nose, and whilst I encircled him with my left arm, I threatened with the right to fling into the river whoever dared come near us with hostile intention. Twenty strong clenched fists let fly at me. I accepted the unequal struggle with superior numbers, and they soon perceived that they had to do with an antagonist, at least much surpassing any single one of them in strength.... I resisted till my call for assistance brought up some Jews who fetched the watch. The wild troop dispersed on their arrival with a loud shout, and I carried, though myself bleeding from many wounds, the fainting boy to the door of his house. The boy was your father dear Schlome; Carpel Sachs, son of the wealthy Beer Sachs.--Arrived at home, as soon as I had told my father what had happened, I fell down and fainted.... My father poured some drops from a flask into my wounds, kissed the blood from my face and smiled kindly.--I was well again, I was happy! Next Friday the wealthy Reb Beer Sachs sent me a beautiful new Sabbath-dress and three gold-pieces, but the present was resolutely refused. The little Carpel had, in consequence of the fright and the ill usage he had been exposed to, been obliged to keep his bed for a week. The first time that he was allowed to leave the house he came to thank me. The tears in his eyes, the profound gratitude, the beautiful words with which the dear boy knew how to give such a true and warm expression of this feeling, won my heart. Carpel asked if he might often visit us, and as my father had no objection to make, Carpel came to us as often as he had time, and a firm bond of love and friendship was knitted between us, in which my brother, also a noble-looking handsome boy took the warmest sympathy. Carpel looked upon me, not unjustly, as his preserver, and his to a certain extent respectful behaviour towards me, that he kept up even to old age, caused almost the only difference in our kindly intercourse. On the occasion of his frequent visits he not unseldom took part in our lessons, and on his side only regretted that we, my brother and I, could not make up our minds to come to his house; but the present of the wealthy Reb Beer Sachs, who had never considered it necessary to thank me in person for the real service which I had rendered his son, had wounded us too deeply; and so it happened, that he scarcely knew his son's preserver by sight.

"We boys spent our time monotonously and quietly, our life was now made beautiful by the love of our little friend Carpel. But on a sudden the hardest blow that could befall us, destroyed our calm happiness. It was that feast of atonement when I and my brother, as we should in a few days be thirteen years old; were fasting for the first time. The day was declining, the departing sunbeams cast their red light, that gradually faded before the advancing darkness, through the lofty narrow windows of the Old-Synagogue, and the tapers were already dimly burning. A profound silence prevailed in the vast space filled with worshippers, when my father stepped to the desk to offer the appointed evening prayer. I myself, though weary and excited, leant against the marble enchased wall which incloses the steps that lead up to the tabernacle in order to look my father in the face as I listened. He was a wonderfully glorious man and at that moment was like an angel. Thus had my childish spirit pictured the Prophet Elias!--His form was tall and unbowed. The dark beard, but scantily sprinkled with grey, fell down upon his breast and curved strikingly upwards against the long white robe, while the locks of his hair, which forced their way from under his turban, were already shining in the silvery glimmer. His noble face now bore a stamp of the deepest devotion, and over his flashing eyes, whose glance kindled enthusiasm, there glowed a dark purple flame in the centre of his forehead. The prayers on the day of atonement are striking, but in my father's mouth they made an extraordinary impression. He did not look into the prayer-book that laid open before him, but gazed heavenwards, so that it seemed as if what he was saying came from the inspiration of the moment, as if he was a divinely inspired seer. Every word that sounded with the full melody of his voice from his lips penetrated victoriously and irresistibly into the hearts of all present. As he repeated the confession of sins with agitating expressiveness all were melted into tears, and when on the other hand he gave utterance in prayer to a devout trust in God's mercy, all felt exalted and strengthened. At length he came to the end. With pious confidence in God he intoned seven times at the top of his voice: 'The everlasting is our

God' and as the thousand voiced loud chorus of all who were present broke magnificently against the vault of God's temple, my father sank suddenly down:--I caught him in my arms....

"'I die,' he said in a feeble but audible voice. 'Lord of this world! my father dared to breathe his life away upon the scaffold for the glory of Thy holy name.--Me Thou hast not accounted worthy of this favour.... but Thou permittest me to die here, on holy ground, reconciled to Thee, at the conclusion of the festival of atonement.--Father of all I thank thee!'--then he signed to my brother also to draw near him, and said in faint dying voice that grew ever weaker and weaker: 'My children, time presses.... Your mother rests in the grave at Cologne.... In Prague, as attendant in this consecrated house, I have passed the loveliest most tranquil years of my life.... Love one another.... sorrow not, despair not!... What God doeth that is well done.... this world is but the vestibule of the next, bear this ever in mind, and some day *on your own deathbeds inculcate it on your children*--a benediction--a faint 'Hear oh Israel,' and the noble man was no more!

"The day but one after we stood weeping at his grave as we returned to our now desolate house, I asked my brother: 'What shall we do now?' The sensible boy fixed his bright eyes upon me. 'Didst thou not hear what our father said at his decease? Your mother lies buried in Cologne ... We have prayed to-day at our father's grave, shall we not also visit the last resting-place of our dear forsaken mother?'

"'Yes, yes dear, brother,' I cried, casting myself with loud sobs on his breast, 'to Cologne, to Cologne, to our mother's grave.'

"During the seven days of mourning we arranged that directly after the feast of tents we would start on our long journey. To our single friend the little Carpel we made known our intention to his deep and infelt regret. Tears rose in the poor boy's eyes, but he repressed them like a man, that he might not vex us still more. On the feast of Tabernacles we both, my brother and I, kept our 13th birthday. It was just the day on which expositions are made. We attended the early service and got ourselves called upon to expound. Then we went to the burial ground, where the rulers of the Old-synagogue had caused a handsome gravestone to be erected to my father, on which a bunch of grapes and the symbols of a Levite were chiselled.... and then with slender bundle on back and staff in hand went forth from the gate. Carpel accompanied us for an hour. He pressed a small purse into the hand of each of us, and assured us, that it consisted entirely of his own savings and that he had said nothing to his father about this present. Then we renewed once more our covenant of eternal friendship....

"'Forget me not, dear friends,' said Carpel as he took farewell.... 'Mosche! I thank thee once more; we are still boys, but shall some day be men, do not forget, Mosche; that in Prague you have a friend, whose life you have saved, who is for ever thy debtor, who is prepared every moment of his life to pay the heavy debt.... Forget me not, as I will never forget thee! Carpel kissed me, my brother, then flung himself once more sobbing aloud on my breast. Exerting all the force of my soul I at length tore myself away.... We set off, Carpel sat himself down upon a hillock and gazed weeping after us.... He was very sorry for us.... We were so lonely, so forsaken. Father and mother lying in the grave, and our one faithful little friend staying behind in despair!--Ignorant of the road we wandered over all Germany. We experienced many a sorrow, many a pain, but were sometimes entertained compassionately and sympathetically. After a difficult journey of many months we at length arrived at the end of our travel, at Cologne. Our hearts beat high as we passed through the city-gate. But the unwonted fatigues of the long way, had exhausted my brother's strength, and the poor boy fell down, sick and worn out, in the open street. I was alone with him in a strange city, my burning eyes sought help despairingly--then God sent us a preserver. An elderly gentleman stepped out of the house on the threshold of which my brother was lying unconscious.

"'A sick child in the open street?' he enquired, 'who is the boy?'

"'It is my brother,' I answered shyly, 'we are orphans, we have come from far away out of Bohemia, to visit our mother's grave....'

"'Carry the boy into the room upstairs,' was the gentleman's order, 'lay him in bed, let him have some broth, I will attend to him directly....'

"'We are Jew-boys, gracious Sir,' I cried quickly.

"'I too am a Jew,' smiled the worthy man, 'I am Baruch Süss, favourite physician to our gracious Elector, the Archbishop of Cologne.'"

Gabriel shuddered but read on:--

"Bustling servants carried my sick brother up the broad stairs into a splendidly furnished room and laid him in bed. I stayed with my brother. The noble humane Baruch Süss examined him with the greatest attention and found that he was lying sick of an inflammatory fever, that he probably would require nothing but complete repose, and that it would not be possible to form a decided opinion as to the further progress of the disorder till after a lapse of one and twenty days.--Suddenly fresh childs' voices were heard at the door, which was pulled open and two lovely maidens peeped into the room. The roguish smile on their face rapidly yielded to the deepest emotion, as their father enjoined silence by a sign, and informed them in a low voice that they must give up their room for the present to a poor parentless boy, who had fallen suddenly ill in the street. *The two maidens were the daughters of Baruch Süss, Miriam and Perl.*"

The manuscript escaped from Gabriel's nervously trembling hand. Must the memory of his grandfather, of his mother, just to-day, in the hour when, obstinately advancing, he wished to cut off the last possibility of retreat, must it just to-day be awakened in him in such a strange, unexpected, he was obliged reluctantly to admit, in such an almost miraculous manner? Was he perhaps to discover in this writing, that a curious accident had played into his hands at a critical moment, a solution of the mystery of his birth? And if he did find it, should he account all these remarkable coincidences as chance, or rather as a wonderful proof of that all powerful providence which he had often so defiantly challenged? These thoughts assailed Gabriel with all the compass of their fearful import, and worked upon him all the more effectually, as the tide of the swiftly succeeding events of the day was calculated to shake the strongest determination. He paced impetuously up and down the room. "I must not read further," he muttered to himself, "till I have embraced a resolution. If I should find a disclosure about my father in this manuscript, if I durst hope that he would fold me in his arms, that he would press me lovingly to his breast, Gabriel, what in the whole past, what in the future would matter unto you? If I could find my father, if I could find him such as I have always pictured him to myself in the short moments of blissful dreams, if such I could fold him in my arms--though it were but for the most infinitesimal instant of time that the human mind can conceive--*God*!"

Gabriel's passionate excitement had attained a height that may easily be imagined. In the most violent excess of a feeling that eagerly sought an escape he had uttered the word, that, at least in his self-communings, had not passed his lips for a long series of years, and he almost shuddered, as the strange sound fell, if involuntarily, almost believingly from his mouth....

"But if he be dead, and gone," cried Gabriel, looking up suddenly almost joyfully, "if I should learn precisely out of this manuscript, that he is irrecoverably lost to me.... if then no other tie than vengeance, continues to bind me to this life, *then, then,* ... my purpose remains immoveable."

He sat down, and his eyes could not fly over the somewhat faded characters with sufficient swiftness. He read on:--

"My brother was taken the best care of. Death had once ravished from our benefactor Baruch Süss two hopeful boys in one week. These boys must have been of about our age, and this circumstance heightened the sympathy that his noble heart felt for us, especially for my sick brother.--It happened just as Baruch Süss had prophesied. For three weeks my brother lay in fever and delirium: on the twenty first day he dropped for the first time into a profound and peaceful slumber. Süss waited for the sick child's waking with almost fatherly compassion. At length my poor brother to my inexpressible delight opened his beautiful dark eyes, raised himself in bed, and looked about him in wonderment. 'Where are we? Mosche!' he asked in a feeble trembling voice. I threw myself passionately on to his neck and my tears bedewed his pale sunken cheeks.

"'Thou hast been ill, poor child,' said Süss, 'God has permitted thy recovery, thou must be grateful to him.'

"I related with an overflowing feeling of gratitude, with how much goodness our benefactor had behaved towards us, and as my brother seized the noble man's hand in deep emotion, pressed it to his quivering lips, and vainly struggled after words to express his heartfelt thanks, a strange convulsive movement passed over the face of Süss, and his eyes filled with tears.... 'You are dear good boys!' he said, profoundly agitated.... The memory of his two early lost sons may have combined with the warm sympathy of his own great heart. He hurried out of the room, that he might not depress the spirits of the convalescent by his unwonted emotion. We remained alone. At this moment we felt ourselves infinitely calmed, we did not stand any longer so entirely alone, so entirely forsaken! Süss allowed the convalescent to take fresh air in the garden attached to his house, and it was there, that we became better acquainted with his daughters. They were probably rather younger than ourselves. Both of them, but especially Miriam the elder, had been endowed with the most excellent natural gifts. Their extraordinary and, especially for maidens of their age, almost unparalleled beauty most perfectly harmonised with a subtle, comprehensive, deeply penetrating intellect, with a disposition that seemed formed to be a shining example to youthful womanhood. The friendly, confiding, almost sisterly behaviour of the girls which their good father manifestly approved of, made a profound, inerasable impression upon us.

"So long as my brother was not quite recovered, we dared not think of accomplishing the aim of our journey, of visiting our mother's grave. It cost me a severe struggle, not to hasten alone to the burial ground, but it would have vexed my poor brother, and I loved him so fervently!

"At last he was strong enough.... we walked out to the burial ground. Our father had given us a sufficient description of the stone that covered our mother's grave; we found it easily, and the long desired aim of our journey was reached. The frame of mind in which we found ourselves I cannot paint to you, my dear children? The most reverential fear, the most sorrowful emotion seized powerfully hold of our young minds.... We prayed long and softly, and when at length we were forced to tear ourselves away in order to return home, we flung ourselves with loud sobs into each other's arms. 'We have no father, no mother, ...' said my brother, deeply moved. 'I have only thee, thou hast only me!--I will love thee for ever, for ever, I will never forsake thee, never! Brother, love me too, as I love thee!...'

"I could not answer from excitement. I folded him impetuously to my loud-beating heart, and pressed my hot lips to his pale forehead, on which at that instant a bright streak of flame was burning. The firm bond of brotherly love was to be knitted if possible still more closely, the beautiful covenant was anew concluded, in a sacred hour, in a spot that was infinitely holy to us children!

"'What will you do now?' asked Süss, when we returned, grave and agitated, to his house. This question surprised us. Since our father's death we had entertained no other thought, could not have grasped any other thought than to pray at our mother's grave. It had so entirely filled our young minds, had kept our spirits in such perpetual excitement, that we had not even for a moment considered what was to come after, that we now for the first time cast a scrutinising look upon our future. We stood with downcast eyes for a while in silence before Süss. My brother recovered himself first. 'What do we propose to do?' he repeated.--'Before anything else to render thanks to you, dear benefactor, for your inexpressible goodness, for the kindness, for the fatherly affection that you have devoted to us poor forsaken orphans in such abundant measure, to thank you for tending me a poor boy, and with God's assistance healing me in a sore sickness--to thank you, ye dear good girls for your compassion, for that ye were not proud towards the poor stranger boys, that you weeped when I was sick and rejoiced, when the good God let me recover,--for that you were kind to us as sisters, you rich beautiful maidens to us poor, poor boys!' ... and next he continued after a short pause during which he strove to overcome his deep emotion, and swallowed with an effort his hot tears, next we shall pursue our journey, go to some school, study God's word, and endeavour to become worthy of our father Reb Jizchok Meduro, to become worthy of our grandfather, who ended his life heroically upon the scaffold, in remembrance of whom the fiery mark sparkles on our forehead in moments of sanctification!'

"My brother ceased; he was glorious to look upon, his eyes flashed beaming with soul, and the fiery mark of which he spoke, even then rose splendidly and contrasted with the pale, still somewhat sickly, child's face, with the pure forehead white as alabaster.--I gazed with a sad fraternal pride on my twin-brother, who seemed to draw his words in strange wise out of his breast. The two girls sobbed softly, and Baruch Süss required some time to collect himself.

"'I will not let you go, you dear fine boys,' he cried, 'never, no never God forbid that I should let you go out into the wide world, forsaken, orphaned. Seeing that a fortunate dispensation caused you to cross my threshold, you must now remain with me. I too had once two beautiful good boys.... The Lord hath taken them from me. Will you supply their place to me? Will you be my sons, will you be the brothers of these girls?'

"This unlooked for offer took us by surprise. The blissful feeling that we had suddenly, unexpectedly, found a new home struggled with an innate proud reluctance to accept a benefit for which we could make no return save our boundless gratitude.--We wavered for an instant and knew not what reply to make; but when Miriam grasping our hands with tearful eye and trembling voice implored us not to go away, to stay with her father--it seemed to us as if no opposition could be thought of; we stayed.

"Baruch Süss treated us ever with fatherly kindness, and we always succeeded in preserving his favour. Our late father had already initiated us in the study of God's word, and so it came to pass, that in spite of our youth we had soon made rapid progress. In the house of Süss we had now full leisure to indulge in our wonted occupations. All our wants were cared for in the kindest manner, and we soon felt as much at home as in the house of our parents--Baruch Süss was besides so good as to let us be instructed in those sciences, of which our father in the tenderest years of our boyhood had only been able to give us the first indications. His exertions in our favour had the best consequences. The examples of our forefathers continually hovered before our souls, and urged us to the greatest industry, to the highest sacrifices. We were soon proposed as a brilliant pattern to the Jewish youth, not only in Cologne, but in the whole Rhine-country--our names were every where mentioned with distinction, and Baruch Süss felt himself thereby richly rewarded. We lived happily and contentedly, and grew up.--I may now when all that is over say so--two splendid youths, equally well developed in mind and body, while Miriam and Perl blossomed into exquisitely lovely young women.

"I had arrived at the age, when the heart willingly opens to love. Miriam's infinite attractiveness, the enrapturing grace of her demeanour, her noble heart, her wonderfully penetrating mind, had made a powerful, ineffaceable impression upon me, an impression that soared to the height of love. I did not make the slightest attempt to conquer this noble passion. Miriam's most friendly kindest sympathy did not permit me to regard my bold hopes as unattainable, the less that Baruch Süss too, when we became young men, made no difference in his domestic economy, allowed us to make use of the intimate 'Thou' to his daughters, and recognised our deserts with almost fatherly affection.--His immense wealth, his influence, his position at the electoral court, made it moreover possible for him in the choice of his sons-in-law to neglect the petty considerations which so frequently stand in the way of the dearest wishes. I rocked myself in dreams of a happy glad future, but I avoided giving expression to these sweet dreams and my hopes remained for months a secret even to my dear and infinitely loved brother, to my brother whom in fact I loved more than myself! At length it seemed to me treachery against my fraternal affection, if I should any longer preserve silence with respect to a feeling that struck daily deeper root in my soul. We occupied a room in common, and in the dusk of a fading summer's day I opened my heart to him. I held my arms twined about his neck, and leant my head on his cheeks. It seemed to me, as if he suddenly shivered and began to tremble; but I convinced myself that it was a delusion, and as he gazed for a long while fixedly before him, I thought, that liveliest sympathy for me had plunged him into a deep reverie. I sought to read his features, but the increasing darkness made this impossible. 'Art thou then convinced that Miriam loves thee?' he enquired at length in a dull voice. I had often put the same question to myself, and ever given it an answer favourable to myself, and Miriam's behaviour justified me in doing so; but I forgot that she behaved exactly in the same way to my brother, and it was only the later unfavourable turn, which this connection, that at first caused me so much happiness, took, which directed my attention to that fact, without however my being ever able to fully make out the real state of the case: and even to this day, when manifold experiences have increased my knowledge of human nature, I cannot say for certain whether Miriam then loved me or my brother, or whether her virgin heart hovered in anxious timorousness between us. At that time I believed that I could answer my brother's question with an honest yes. The dejected silence into which my brother sunk anew, was equally misunderstood by me, I thought that I saw therein only an excessive fear lest Baruch Süss should refuse me his daughter's hand. I remained but a short time involved in this error; I was suddenly bitterly undeceived. Some days afterwards I awoke in the night and heard a loud and violent talking and weeping in my room. I sprung swiftly from my couch. It was a clear starlight night, and the pale moonlight fell just upon my brother's bed--he, as was often the case with him, was talking in his dreams. The sorrow, that was printed on the sleeper's face, the large tears, that welled from under his closed lashes and rolled over his pale cheeks, filled me for a moment with a strange pensive grief; but I soon smiled at my childish pity. I would wake him, scare away the evil dream, that enchained his mind--but as I was about to call him, there fell on my soul, as it were a quivering flash of lightning, followed by a roaring thunderclap, and the words which escaped slowly from his lips became on a sudden clear and transparent.--I listened with restrained breath.

"'I love my dear brother more than life,' he said, 'and he loves Miriam!... Hush, Hush! No one shall hear of it, but Thou, my God and Lord; Thou that beholdest my writhing, lacerated heart.... I will be silent, silent as the grave for ever.... not Miriam, not my brother, no man shall hear of it.... Oh! indeed I am glad, brother! dear brother, take Miriam for thy bride.... and, I can surely die! I will not trouble the joy of your wedding day, I will not weep.... No! I will be glad and laugh at your happiness, will laugh so right heartily, as on my brother's day of rejoicing, on the wedding day of him whom I most ardently love.... Oh, mine is no forced laugh, I laugh so truly from my whole heart; see--ha, ha, ha!...'

"But my brother did not laugh, but sobbed convulsively. My heart contracted frightfully, an indescribable, almost physically painful grief thrilled through me--I could not at first speak for maddening sorrow, but then cried aloud, casting myself upon the bed of my sleeping brother: 'no, dear one, no, thou shalt not give her up.... Miriam shall be thine.... thine, thine, for ever.'

"My brother awoke.--What I said, showed him clearly, that I was acquainted with his heart's secret. I lay upon his breast sobbing aloud.

"'A woman, dear brother!' he began at length with trembling voice vainly striving for composure--'a woman, though it were the glorious Miriam, shall not divide our hearts. Thee only I possessed in the wide world, thou wert my all, brother! Dost yet remember, how thou, thyself sick and weary, didst carry me in thy arms, when on our journey to the mother's grave I had wounded my foot? Dost yet remember, how thou didst watch at my sick-bed for three weeks together, and didst scarcely get any sleep? Dost yet remember, how our dying father exhorted us to love one another? Dost yet remember, how we renewed the covenant at our mother's grave?--And do you think that I, that I have forgotten all that, all that? No, brother: take thou Miriam to wife.... be happy!

"A noble strife arose between us. Each of us wished to give up with bleeding heart, and neither would accept the sacrifice offered by fraternal love.--The most curious, the strangest ideas, such as could only be born of so desperate a situation, danced in rapid succession before us.--Lot, Miriam herself should decide; but they were rejected as fast as entertained. At last a manly resolution the fruit of a long painful struggle ripened in us: *we would both give her up*. Neither of us should possess Miriam, and our love should remain a secret for ever. In our mutual passionate brotherly love we determined to forget the infinite sorrow that filled us.--

"We wished, we were bound to leave the house at daybreak, to which the mightiest ties enchained us. On the next day we stood pale, confused, with tears in our eyes before our friend Süss who had loved us as a father, and declared to him with hesitating voice our suddenly formed resolution of leaving his house, of proceeding farther on our journey. Süss was alarmed, he glared at us speechlessly, our fixed purpose seemed to have overthrown one of his favourite schemes. He vainly endeavoured to detain us, fruitlessly enquired the reason that had caused us to take a step so unexpected. 'Stay with me, I have good designs for you....' repeated Süss over and over again sadly, and when he saw how immovably we remained true to our purpose, he said at length painfully subduing his pride: 'Stay with me, be my sons.... I have only daughters, two lovely glorious daughters.... but I wish also to have two sons.... Will you not be my sons? My daughters, I have good ground for thinking so, are affectionately disposed towards you....' Süss said no more, his parental pride struggled with his parental love.--To us it was clear that Süss had intended to make choice of us as his sons-in-law, and that his daughters had fully shared the wish. I and my brother, as twins usually are, were almost exactly like one another, for which of us would Miriam have decided? A painful torturing pause ensued. Süss could not divine the real reason, why we who had entered his house as poor orphan boys, despised his exquisitely graceful daughters, the loveliest, wealthiest, noblest maidens among the German Jews. We, my brother and I, needed all the strength of our manhood, not to succumb to the unutterable pain of despair. One of us must of necessity be standing close to that hotly desired aim, that we both, each with the fullest force of his will, were striving to attain--and now to be obliged to draw back, to be obliged to draw back in silence, and by so doing to inflict an injury perhaps mortal on him whom we loved beyond measure--that thought annihilated us.

"Süss, wounded in the most sensitive place of his heart, in his pride as a father, was profoundly mortified. 'I cannot and must not detain you any longer,' he said with bitter grief.... 'Go!... may you never repent having thus departed.' Then he stepped hastily to the door and said with an accent that rent our hearts: 'Oh, would that you had never crossed the threshold of my house!...'

"We would not thus separate from our benefactor. We hastened after him to his room--it was closed against us: We sent by an old servant of the house to ask that we might as a favour be allowed to take farewell of his daughters, it was refused us. We almost succumbed to the unutterable grief of despair..... On the evening of that same day we proposed to leave Cologne, the inexhaustible goodness of Süss furnished us with an abundant outfit for our further journey--but he would never see us again. At night-fall we got into the travelling carriage, that waited for us at the back door of the house. We cast a sorrowful look at the window of that room which Miriam occupied.... two maiden faces looked forth into the gathering twilight, and the violent trembling of one of them, who pressed her handkerchief to her eyes, showed that she was sobbing impetuously--it was Miriam!

"Our hearts beat audibly, my brother's beautiful features were frightfully disfigured, he must have suffered as unutterable woe as I did.--I gazed into his face, visibly convulsed with sorrow. 'Brother,' I said, 'there is yet time.... I can renounce.... do thou return to Miriam. If Miriam wavers between us both, or even if she loves but one of us, thy return will be decisive in thy favour.... Thou, Miriam, our benefactor Süss, you all will be happy....'

"'And thou?' asked my brother in a tone of the woefullest reproach.

"'I go far away and strive to forget....' I tried hard to answer, but my voice shook, and tears rolled irrestrainably over my cheeks. My brother fell sobbing into my arms.--'I will never forsake thee, Brother!' he cried--'good brother! cast me not away from thy noble heart.'

"We went from one school to another; our name was already known far and wide, we met with a friendly reception everywhere: but we felt nowhere at home. We never mentioned Miriam, but the memory of this hapless love threw a gloom over our life. We plunged with unwearied industry into the study of God's word, we increased our stores of knowledge, but the thorn in our bleeding hearts did not therefore pain us the less.... We had acquired in the Talmudic world an unheard of renown for students, we were often honoured by letters from illustrious Rabbis, who desired our advice, our opinion upon scientific religious questions. The most important Rabbinates were offered to us, we might have obtained the highest aim of a Talmud-student. But neither of us could do so. Memory still drove us unquietly from place to place.

"A year had elapsed since our departure from Cologne, when in one of our wanderings we happened to hear that the younger daughter of the wealthy electoral physician Süss had given her hand to her cousin Joel Rottenberg of Worms, while the elder had previously absolutely refused to enter into the bond of matrimony. This news filled both of us with a strange sensation of sadness. To each of us, though he dared not allow it to himself--a ray of hope seemed to dawn:--and yet neither of us would have been made happy without the other. Once more, for the last time I asked my brother whether he would return to Miriam; but he saw my soul's infinite sorrow, after a short violent struggle his fraternal affection conquered, he stayed with me; we would never separate:

"Another year elapsed, we were then living in Germersheim, a community not far from Spires. We had in the course of our short residence there won the approval and respect of the Rabbi, and when he died soon after our arrival, he enjoined the community upon his death-bed to elect one of us as his successor, and it besieged us with petitions that one of us would accept the vacant chair of the Rabbi; and marry the daughter of the defunct who lived with her now widowed mother. I was still in no mood to accept these offers, however attractive and honourable they might be; my brother also decidedly refused them. We determined therefore to withdraw ourselves from all further discussion by a distant journey. I was busily occupied in my little room in the house of the Rabbi's widow packing my effects for the journey, when my brother suddenly entered. He was pale as a corpse, his looks were troubled.

"'Do you know what a foreign student has just been relating *in the lecture-room*?'

"'What?'

"'Miriam Süss has at length yielded to her father's entreaty and given her hand to her cousin Joseph Süss of Spires.--The wedding was solemnised magnificently at Cologne.'--

"I felt a warm sympathy for my brother; at that moment I perceived for the first time that he was of a more passionate nature than I. The heavy blow, which I had expected for years, came upon him like a thunderbolt out of a blue sky. He fell upon a chair, in vain he pressed his hands to his face, the tears welled out between his fingers.

"'But brother, brother,' I cried, myself struggling to keep down all the recollections and thoughts that awoke within me, couldest thou have expected anything else? Why troublest thou thyself? What can it now signify to thee? be a man, brother, be strong!'

"'God!' sobbed my brother, 'could I have known that!... could I have known that Miriam would be so weak as to forget me! oh! brother, brother, believe me, Miriam loved only me, me and none else, she could love no one, as she loved me! oh, I made a great, an infinitely great, sacrifice to thee, when I gave her up, *fruitlessly gave her up* to thee!... oh! why wert thou not magnanimous, why didst thou accept this sacrifice?'

"I looked into my brother's face with the deepest grief, I had never seen him so passionate, so excited before, and yet I thought that I knew him as well as myself, for was he not my twin-brother. It seemed to me almost as if at that moment the dark night of madness was shadowing his clear spirit. The fire in his eyes sparkled wildly and weirdly.

"'Thou hast made a fruitless sacrifice of thyself to me?' I repeated painfully agitated: 'did I desire it, did I wish for it?--and I, I? dost think my heart is of stone? dost think that I have suffered less than thou, because I have said nothing? I too have often screamed in the bitter agony of my soul, as I watched in despair through the long melancholy night.--Consider, brother! I, I do not reproach thee.'

"I suffered inexpressibly: the news, which again painfully tore open my heart's wounds, joined to the passionate unjust reproaches of my brother, whom I loved so tenderly, by whom I believed that I was so tenderly loved, agitated my mind with such violence that I fell dangerously ill. For eight weeks I strove with the angel of death. In the confused wild fever dreams of my sickness it sometimes seemed to me as if an angel approached my couch, as if a girl's white hand touched my burning forehead--once I thought, that a lovely woman bent over my bed and that a tear rolled down upon my face.--God--praised be his name--granted my recovery. He refreshed me with the springs of his infinite grace. The sickness had had the most beneficial, the most inexplicable influence upon my life. A new fresh stream of blood seemed to roll through my veins. I was restored not only to bodily, but also to mental health. My love for Miriam, now the wife of another, which I must have violently eradicated, had died out in a miraculous manner. Oh yes, it was a miracle! and I thanked God for that instance of his goodness!--The noble handsome girl who had nursed me with more than a sister's care, who had watched night after night by my bed, full of sympathy and compassion, was thy mother, dear Schöndel.--Leah the daughter of the Rabbi's widow.... Thy mother was lovely and good. As long as Miriam had reigned in my heart, I had not noticed the wonderfully beautiful maiden, but now, that I was once more free, my earnest gratitude was easily converted into an infelt, fervent, faithfully returned love. Half a year after my convalescence Leah became my wife, and I took my seat in the Rabbi's chair at Germersheim.

"During my sickness my brother had shown me the most self-sacrificing love, and had attached himself again to me with the greatest tenderness, as though to make me forget the inauspicious reproach that had pained me so much. I had never borne ill will against him. True it is that he had shaken with rude hand the firm bonds, that held our hearts entwined, that the hasty word which he had uttered, had touched me to the quick,--but, dear children! you do not know what brotherly love is, you do not know, how one loves a brother, and above all a twin-brother!... From our birth, from our mother's lap we had been united to one another by the sweetest holiest bonds.--The same pulsation had stirred our hearts, we had lain on the same mother's breast, we had hitherto fairly and equally shared every sorrow and every joy.--I could not help it, I was constrained to love my brother with undiminished cordiality!

"In the first year of a happy peaceful marriage thy mother presented me with an admirably beautiful girl, with thee, dear Schöndel.... I was happy, but my happiness endured but for a short time; eight days after your birth thy dear never to be forgotten mother died! You may conceive my profound grief! I formed a firm immoveable resolution never to marry again, and following my father's lofty example to dedicate my whole life to the study of God's word, to the religious care of my community, to the education of my only beloved child.--In the conscientious performance of my duties I at length found tranquillity, and when thou, Schöndel, didst gaze at me with thy sweet child-like smile, when thou didst extend to me thy little delicate hands, I felt myself almost happy!

"My brother was my faithful companion. He occupied a small room in my house and studied almost the whole of the day. My heart was filled with the sad remembrance of my deceased wife, so soon snatched from me. I never thought of Miriam except with a sensation of friendly gratitude. Every feeling of love for her.--I have already said so--had quite died out in me. I could have calmly conversed with my brother about her father and sister: but I did not dare to do so, because the profound silence which he preserved, was an unmistakeable sign, that he had not yet conquered his once deep felt love, that it still remained rankling with full strength in his soul. Miriam's name therefore never again crossed our lips. Many advantageous offers of marriage were proposed to my brother, he was elected as Rabbi by many important German communities: but he firmly refused everything, and paid no attention to my well meaning advice.... We often sat all day together, plunged in the study of the Talmud. Once we were engrossed in the solution of a case that had been laid before me for my decision by two Rabbis, who could not come to an agreement with respect to it. We had long remained seated, then in the eagerness of discussion began walking round the room, and at last, as was often the case, happened to stop before the open window. My brother was just on the point of controverting a proposition that I had laid down, when he cast a glance through the window.... He instantly became dumb, his arms fell powerlessly by his side, his lips moved convulsively, but emitted no sound.

"'What ails thee, brother?' I asked in terror.

"He made no answer, but stretched out his arms and pointed to the street; I saw a lady, stepping out of a travelling carriage.

"'What ails thee, brother?' I repeated more earnestly 'I see nothing that can have discomposed you to such a degree.'

"My brother gazed fixedly at me, as if he thought my question an incomprehensible one, then pointed once more at the lady and collecting all his strength, screamed involuntarily in a loud shrill voice: 'Miriam Süss!' and trembling convulsively fell down pale as a corpse. My brother did not come to himself till late in the evening. He was right, it was Miriam. Joseph Süss her husband, had a lawsuit with the magistracy of the city of Spires, and wished to wait for the issue of it at the adjacent town of Germersheim. His wife had followed him. I felt sorry that Joseph Süss had selected just Germersheim for his residence, not for my own but for my brother's sake.

"I did not venture to talk to my brother about Miriam's presence; the sight of her had too much affected him. I made a slight attempt to advise him to go a journey while her stay lasted in Germersheim; but his eyes flashed, as he answered: 'Brother, I have no one in the wide world save thee! I have sacrificed everything, the dearest thing on earth, to thee, cast me not away from thy presence!'

"After a time he became gradually calmer, and I was already beginning to indulge a hope, that he had reconciled himself to his immutable destiny, when after the expiration of some months his behaviour again altered in a strange and striking way. My brother avoided my society, came to me seldomer and seldomer, till at last he shut himself up in his room, and refused either to see me or speak to me. I did not know how to explain this to myself, and only waited a convenient opportunity, to have a private conversation with him. This I at length found, I was usually the first in God's house, and as a rule unlocked its doors. One morning, it was winter. I stepped into the dark and quite empty interior, shortly afterwards the iron gates grated again and a form appeared on the steps that led into the inner synagogue. The pale trembling light of the lamp that ever burneth revealed to me my brother. He stopped irresolutely, as if he would avoid an interview with me alone. I did not give him time to take a resolution, stepped quickly up to him and held out my hand to him. But his hand trembled in mine, he could not bear my steadfast gaze, his eye, that once was wont to look me truly and honestly in the face, remained fixed on the ground, and even his features formerly so beautiful seemed to me marred and disfigured. The red streak of flame on his forehead burned to a deeper hue than had ever been seen on him before, broad violet coloured circles were stamped under his glistening eyes, his blue lips quivered incessantly, it was clear, that my poor brother could not encounter my looks. I gazed into his face, a profound inexpressible pang, an incommunicable sympathy seized my heart:--but then suddenly a ray of conviction flashed across me, brotherly love sharpened my spiritual eyes; Miriam was in Germersheim, her husband was absent, my brother loved her with a furious passion.... his face bore the Cains-mark of guilt, there was no doubt, *my poor brother had sore sinned!* I let fall his hand! I was too violently agitated, and vainly struggled a long time for a word.... My brother broke the painful death-like stillness that reigned in the broad space with no sound. It was a silent confession to me of his guilt!

"Pious worshippers now began to enter into the temple, and I could say no more to him at present; in the deep silence of night, alone, I determined that he should hear his brother's warning voice.

"I passed the day in a state of most painful excitement. Had my brother's bleeding corpse been laid torn and disfigured at my feet I should not have so profoundly mourned him! Could I with the last drop of my heart's blood have undone that, which I now felt myself constrained to admit as certain,--I would have gladly shed it. It was for me to raise again my brother, my poor fallen brother, out of the bottomless depths to which he had sunk. It was for me to tear him from the strong arm of sin; I knew, that it must have been a hard struggle in which my brother was subdued....

"After midnight.... all around was sunk in deep sleep--I crept to the door of his room. I knocked at first gently, then louder, no answer followed.--The key of my room also opened this door. It was not till after long hesitation that I crossed the threshold with loud-beating heart. The small lamp, that I carried with me, threw its dull light round about; I stepped to my brother's bed, it was empty.... my brother was not in his room--I sank down in despair; I had in truth before been convinced of my brother's guilt; but the certainty, this horrible certainty that robbed me of every, even the faintest shadow of a hope, seized my heart anew with a grief as terrible as if I had up to that time had not the least presentiment of it! At the very moment, when my fraternal heart was crying out in the depths of its agony, at the very moment when I was prepared to make any sacrifice to save my brother, at that very moment *my brother, my brother,* 'my second I--oh no, more, more;' I had loved him more than myself, I would have sacrificed myself thousands of times for him--was wantoning! at that very moment my brother was wantoning in the arms of an adulterous woman, *of that woman whom I had once idolized with pure chaste fervent love....*

"What was I to do? I must stay, I must wait for him, though my poor heart should break. I seated myself by the table and tried to read a bible by the lamplight: but I could not. Incapable of thought I gazed out through the open window, and made frequent fruitless attempts to collect myself, to ponder over the address with which I proposed to receive my brother. Every second seemed a century, and yet, and yet I would gladly have postponed the painful moment, and yet I trembled sadly at the slightest sound, that the wind made in the passage. I might have sat thus for three long hours that seemed as if they would never end, when I heard a faint rustle, and shortly afterwards a powerful form swung itself through the window. It was my brother.--He remained standing stiff and motionless as a statue before me. At sight of him all my blood flowed back so swiftly and violently to my heart, that I thought that it must indeed burst; a cold shudder crept over my bones, I had half got up, keeping one hand on the open bible, as if I would draw strength and confidence from it. A long pause ensued, it exhausted my nervous system, more than ten years of trouble would have done!

"I had reckoned with certainty that my brother would fall broken-hearted into my arms, that the sight of me at that hour would remind him of all that he had forgotten. I believed that he would come to meet me; but I had deceived myself, my brother remained stiff and motionless and never once dropped his eyes....

"In spite of the immense excitement in which I found myself at this fateful moment, the whole impression of it has continued uneffaced in my memory, and even at this day, when I am writing this history--though almost twenty years have since elapsed,--the image of my poor brother stands with perfect clearness before my soul, the image of my brother, as J saw him then for the last time. He was tall, about the same height as myself, his eyes flashed weirdly under black bushy eyebrows, on his forehead, the fiery sign of our family glowed in deepest purple, his dark beard set off the frightful corpselike pallor of his face, his quivering lips were so violently convulsed that his large moustachios kept continually trembling, his long abundant hair fell in tangled masses over his shoulders."

Gabriel stopped again. From the depths of his soul confused memories all suddenly emerged, that ever became clearer and clearer. That form, which had once pressed its burning lips on the face of the frightened child, stepped life-like before him--a half faded reminiscence of a beggar, who had once followed him in Aix-la-Chapelle from the church door to his house, again gathered life and strength. Strange to say, it now for the first time, after a long series of years had weakened and effaced the impression of these forms, seemed to him, that they resembled each other--that both, Gabriel thought that he could not be mistaken--corresponded with the description of his father. In vain he sought to realise another embodiment of this picture, which he imagined that he had seen only a short time back. But human memory possesses this strange peculiarity, that it is just the impressions of the remotest past, and especially youthful impressions, that survive with greater vividness and clearness, than those, we have received later; and, as the best shot in the heat of battle often misses the nearest aim, in the same way did Gabriel, usually so strong-minded, in his almost mad excitement vainly strive to conjure up this recollection. He hoped perhaps to obtain from what followed more particular discoveries about his father and read on:--

"I was determined to preserve silence, and left it to my brother to break the profound stillness, that could not be less painful to him than to me.... My brother was silent for a long time; his breast laboured fearfully, he breathed heavily, his face too was extraordinarily convulsed as I had never seen it before. The veins on his forehead swelled, as if they would burst, his underlip dropped loosely down, foam gathered on his mouth before he had spoken a word.--I perceived, that he was seeking a word, a thought, wherewith to crush, to annihilate me. I was afraid of him, but nevertheless gazed at him fixedly and steadily. At last after a hard struggle some words escaped from his lips, but his voice sounded hollow and dead: 'What seekest thou here in the dead of night? Why dost thou act as a spy upon me? Art thou my keeper? What dost thou want of me?'

"I had not expected such a stubborn unbending defiance. I stood at first as if turned to stone, but at the next moment my hot Spanish blood immediately boiled over; with a wild passionate excitement, such as one only feels at such a moment, under such circumstances, I answered my brother.

"'Dost thou ask, what I want of thee? Can you dare ask? Can you look me in the face as if you were free and innocent? Do you not sink into the ground for shame? Look into your own breast! Look! your very face bears signs of your wicked wicked deed.... you ask what I want of you? I would save you, tear you from the strong arm of sin, but lo! it holds thee fast in brazen chains!--I stopped, my words seemed ineffectual. My brother's features bore an expression of the wildest fury, he gnashed his teeth, but made no answer.

"'Brother!' I began again, after a short painful pause, 'Brother! hast thou then forgotten everything, everything? Hast thou no more memory for the past, no regard for the future?... Oh, gaze not at me so stonily, as if thou didst not understand me.... Brother, by that infinite love which I have felt for thee, by the memory of our deceased father, by the recollection of our early lost mother upon my knees I implore thee,--think of it, *only think of it*, what a transgression thou hast committed!... Yes! gaze at me as you will, with eyes sparkling with rage, gnash your teeth, clench your fist, I do not tremble, yes! thou hast fearfully sinned, yes, yes! dost hear?'

"I was so immeasurably confounded by my brother's obstinate unexpected resistance, that I could say no more. I grasped at the bible which was lying on the table, opened at the ten commandments and pointed silently at the seventh.

"'Thou shalt not commit adultery!' I recommenced after a deep pause, during which we could hear our hearts beating.... 'Thou shalt not lust after thy neighbour's wife.... Dost thou see, thus it is written, thus was it declared to listening mankind on flaming Sinai!... Well then, that word of God, that word of God, which was a pillar of fire unto thy people illuminating them in the darkness of night, and an ever refreshing fountain in the heat of the day, that word of God, for which thy grandfather endured a death by fire, that word of God whose everlasting truth, thy father, I, every pious Jew, would have sealed with his heart's blood, that same word of God thou hast despised, cast from thee, trampled under foot!... Art thou not acquainted with the sentence of our wisemen. All shall be inheritors of the kingdom to come, all save three, the adulterer, the....'

"I could say no more, a fearful change came over my brother. His features, even before marred and disfigured, now took an expression so frightful, that they scarcely seemed to belong to an human being, all the blood in his face seemed to have gathered into the dark-red borders about his eyes, these protruded in an unnatural size far out of their sockets, his mouth stood wide open, and disclosed his beautiful white teeth--he resembled at that moment a wild blood-thirsty animal.

"'Thou hast robbed me of this world, wilt thou rob me of the next too?' he yelled, after a long pause with a loud howl and threw himself furiously upon me. I perceived to my unutterable grief, that my well meant but bitter word, had penetrated the inmost recesses of his soul, that the consciousness of his guilt had awaked in him with overwhelming force, that it had suddenly conjured up the darkness of madness over his once so clear and luminous mind.... In vain was now my friendly address, he attacked me with the wild fury of delirium. 'Brother! let go, let go, force me not to exert my strength?' I cried, 'we are still brothers, Twin-brothers, I am still thy Mosche!...' But my brother heeded me not, he seized me in his nervous grasp by the neck. My life was in imminent danger. I did not much value life on my own account; but I desired to preserve thy father for thee, dear Schöndel, thou who haddest none other in the wide world but me, and the thought of thee gave me a giant's strength! I had at first vainly more than once endeavoured to force away my brother, whose hand compressed my throat violently, but could not succeed in doing so.... My breathing became difficult, the blood rushed to my head, lights danced before my eyes. I was giddy, I felt that some decided course must be taken, that I must disengage myself from my terrible opponent. I collected all my strength, and forced him with the whole weight of my body to the ground. 'Peace, Mosche,

Peace!' said my brother at last, grinding his teeth, after a fruitless struggle to break from my arms.... let me go, I will be quiet!'

"I trusted his promise, but at the next moment he sprung upon me with the fury and agility of a tiger, fastened his sharp teeth upon my naked breast, and made most desperate efforts to strangle me. I screamed aloud for excess of pain, and seized him, in obedience to a dim instinct of self-preservation, by the throat.... a violent wrench of my sinewy wrist--and my brother with a hollow muttering and distorted visage sunk lifeless down! I stood for an instant in despair, motionless, then threw myself, mad with grief, upon the ground and endeavoured to recall him to life. My exertions were ineffectual!

"I recovered my presence of mind with astonishing rapidity, and it was again the thought of thee, my dear daughter! which drew me out of the wild storm of despair.... I opened the window, and cried out aloud to the star-spangled heaven: '*Lord of the world: Thou hast seen it, Thy paternal eye was watching.... I am not guilty of his death, I am no Cain, my hand did not shed this blood!'"*

Gabriel, exhausted, almost unconscious, ceased reading, and threw the fateful writing far away from him.... The superhuman strength, with which he had hitherto attentively and greedily devoured the faded characters, gave way. The hope of obtaining information about his father, of searching him out, of being able to fold him to his beating, bursting heart, had pervaded him with the wildest, most blissful rapture--and now, now all these hopes were scattered, annihilated; the very name of his father, which, as if intentionally, was not once mentioned in the manuscript, remained unknown to him.--*The more beautiful nobler aim of his life continued to be unattainable by him.* What mattered to him the farther contents of the manuscript? Of what importance to him was it to learn, how Rabbi Mosche in that same night had taken flight with his daughter, to escape the avenging hands of human justice? Of what importance was it to him to learn, how Reb Carpel Sachs had received the old friend of his youth with warm affection? Of what importance was it to him to learn, how Reb Mosche, as attendant in the Old-Synagogue had led a peaceful, contemplative life, how he embraced the firm resolution, to give the hand of his daughter to a man who like himself, like his deceased father, would accept the modest office of attendant in the Old-Synagogue, where far from the busy tumult of the world he could peacefully live for his faith, for his duties: calm and isolated, like his father, like himself, might quietly close a storm tossed life.... What did all this and more signify to Gabriel? Had he not learnt that his father was dead, lost to him for ever--did he not know, that the hot unstilled longing of his soul must remain for ever and ever ungratified, were not the thousand threads, with which his heart hung to the sweetest hope of his life, suddenly painfully snapped!... Gabriel read no further. He sat for a while motionless in his chair. Language has no power to express the tempest of emotion, that whirled through his breast, and it needs the boldest flight of imagination, to picture it even in faint colour to oneself.

"That hope then is vanished!" he said at last after long silence, pressing his hand convulsively on his heart, "that hope is vanished!... *there remains to me then but one, the only aim of my life. Vengeance* ... Mannsfield is still at Pilsen, Blume's destiny is yet in my hands!... I thank thee, chance, thou hast wonderfully led me, thou hast solved the torturing doubt in the most critical moment.... *vengeance is all that is left to me--my resolution continues immoveable!"*

The strokes of the Rathhaus clock proclaimed, that it wanted but two hours to midnight. About this time the gates of the Jews-town were shut. Gabriel got up hastily, armed and enveloped himself in his cloak, then passed his hand slowly over his lofty forehead white as marble, as though violently to compress every new risen thought, and stepped to the door. On the threshold he paused once more plunged in the overflowing tide of thought, and cast a glance over the room that he was leaving for ever. It seemed, as if he could not after all tear himself away so easily from the dwelling, in which his grandfather had ended a life fruitful in stirring incidents, where his father had passed the lovely period of innocent youth.--All at once he manned himself, and hastened with flying steps to the Jews-town.--In the short distance there he met a man, with his cloak drawn close over his face; it was Michoel Glogau; but both were too busied with their own thoughts, and neither remarked the other.

Gabriel arrived just in time; immediately after his entrance the gates of the Jews' quarter were closed.

Chapter VI

The winter of the year 1620 had set in betimes, it was a raw cold night. The sky was hidden by a grey veil of clouds, dissipated at one moment by the breath of the icy north wind, at another as rapidly re-condensed. The roofs were covered with deep snow, the ground was frozen hard and crunched under footsteps. It had already become quiet, the numerous vendors, who cheapened their wares in open street till a late hour, and whose candles and small lamps gave a singularly friendly aspect to the Jews-town, had disappeared, the streets were almost empty, and only here and there a solitary passenger close wrapped in his cloak was seen hastening home, or to the lecture-room.

Gabriel stepped slowly, through the street, stopping almost every minute. He had experienced in his passion-tossed life much mental anguish. Since the day, when he had stood in despair at his mother's dying bed, since the day when Blume had contumeliously rejected his warm earnest and chaste young love, his whole life had been full of pain and torment--and yet it appeared to him, as if he had never been so unhappy, never so unutterably wretched, as now. His future confronted him more fearful and horrible than ever. The fortune of war, which had hitherto fastened itself to his, to his friend Mannsfield's banners, seemed to have vanished with Frederick's overthrow on this day.... The audacious confidence with which he had made himself irresponsible for his abjuration of everything which he had formerly considered dear and sacred had been dissipated by Michoel's ardent words, which had struck him with the full overpowering force of truth at the most critical hour.... His only hope, to discover his father, to press him to his heart, to reconcile himself to him, to his destiny, perhaps to God.... the audacious hope, which had often raised him from the bottomless pit of despair; this one, sweet hope, which had ever, even when he dared not allow it to himself, glimmered in his soul--was dissipated, was annihilated!

In truth it was the crushing intelligence of his father's early death, which now bowed him down under a burden of infinite sorrow, and almost effaced every earlier impression.... His father had never rejected him, as he had so often in moments of wild excitement feared.... His father had perhaps departed out of this life, without any presentiment that his child would one day be dispairingly searching a trace of his path.... And this father he had never known, and should never, never behold, this father whom he had therefore only so madly hated, because he would have so gladly loved him with the whole gigantic power of his soul!

Gabriel stood pensively in the middle of the street. With the strange bitter grief that, self-tormenting, is wont to tear open the most painful wounds of the heart, he endeavoured once more to bring his father's features which his uncle had so vividly described, before his inner eye; but he strove in vain, confused images alone rose up in his soul, pale men with purple blazing marks on their forehead: and all these dim fancies took shape and vanished with the swiftness of thought: all resembled one another--and yet not one of them was the real genuine image.... And as a man is sometimes unable to remember a word that he desires to utter, and yet it is so infinitely near him, that he thinks, he has but to move the tongue, in order to give voice to it, thus Gabriel peered after this image, it seemed so near, it almost hovered over him--and yet he could not realise it.

"That hope is vanished," he said at length in low tones, passing his hand over his forehead--"fix your looks on something else.... The past is unchangeable--the dead are dead.... The grave restores not to the world, the dead never come to life.... *Thy father is dead, he is irrecoverably lost*.... but my vengeance liveth within me, within my breast with a wild hell-fire.... forget the dead, and remember vengeance!"

Gabriel once more assayed, with that admirable suppleness of character that had enabled him to oppose an almost incredible resistance to the bitter blows which had struck him, to withdraw himself from the destructive influence of this vortex of thoughts, to divert his mind from it.... again he sought, as he was often wont to do in moments of highest excitement, some object exterior to himself, that would fix his attention were it but for a short time, and he accounted himself fortunate, as he recognised in a person, who was walking rapidly by him, the Frankfurt student Nochum.

"Good evening," he said, mastering his temper, and with difficulty restraining the ill-will that he could not but feel in the bottom of his heart towards Nochum: "Whither away?"

"I have been with the chief overseer Reb Gadel," answered Nochum, "I had letters of recommendation to him and am in the habit of studying at nights with his son: but they have just been informed, that the Palatine has come over to the Altstadt, bringing the crown and regalia with him, and has signified to the inhabitants of the Altstadt, that he proposes to withdraw from the city at daybreak and leave the field to his victorious antagonists--as you can well fancy, there could be no more talk of study."

"Is this news to be depended upon?" asked Gabriel, after a long pause of reflection.

"It came to the overseer from the most reliable source, and there can be no doubt about it.... however I must ask you to keep the matter secret till morning: it is still unknown to every one else in the Jews-town, and may very well remain so till to-morrow."

Gabriel observed a thoughtful silence. "I am still master of Blume's destiny," he thought, "she still believes that her husband is in my power.... I must make haste.... if I lose the propitious moment for revenge, it is perhaps irrecoverably, for ever lost!"

Nochum misinterpreted Gabriel's silence. He could in truth have no suspicion of the gravity of the intelligence which he had imparted to him, he could have no idea that he was standing by a man, the only hope of whose life had been shortly before annihilated, who designed to take instant vengeance with the full might of hate for the unutterable woe of his whole tormented Past.

"You seem to take a warm interest in public affairs," began Nochum at length, "and I am very glad of it, one finds it so seldom in a student; but here in Prague, at this renowned high-school one meets students, such as one seldom finds elsewhere.--Yesterday for the first time I made the acquaintance of a student, Michoel Glogau; I am only sorry that he is leaving Prague immediately.... I assure you, never has a young man made so deep an impression upon me as he.... We happened to be talking about a bastard, I laid down a proposition which, I willingly allow, I retracted, when Reb Michoel proved to me that it was wrong.... but what an argument he gave, so clear, so eager, so convincing--but what am I telling you this for, I recollect that you were present during the discussion, and must have heard it too. Michoel found the true, correct, view of the case, did he not?"

Gabriel's heart beat high. His soul was pierced by a thousand arrows, and the reawakened memory of Michoel's crushing words poured boiling oil into all these open uncicatrized wounds.

"I too am sorry that I fell in with Michoel Glogau so late," said Gabriel with profound emotion.... "but it was in sooth too late, too late!"

Nochum looked enquiringly at Gabriel. The intense trouble that was expressed by his features and words seemed to him incomprehensible. Gabriel observed this, he was seized with a sudden terror as if he feared that he had betrayed his most secret thoughts.... "Farewell," he cried, after a short pause suddenly breaking off, and hurried as fast as he could through the narrow irregular streets.--Nochum gazed after him for a while in astonishment and then went quietly on his way.

Gabriel did not stop till he had reached Blume's house in the Hahnpass. He looked up to the attic windows, one of them was open in spite of the raw wintry cold, and he thought that he perceived in the obscurity the outline of a woman's form.... His heart beat audibly, he laid his hand on the door-latch, but still stood lost in thought.

"Thus then I stand at the goal," he began speaking to himself, at first in low tones, then louder and louder.... "through a long life of torment I have pined for the moment of revenge.... Now it is come, no power on earth can now interpose between me and my revenge.... I will avenge myself.... and then?... then solitary, forsaken, unwept and unregretted--will die on the nearest battle-field.--It might have been otherwise!... Had I encountered that Michoel, whom I now at the end of my wide, wide wandering have found, had I encountered him on that feast of atonement, had he then said those words, which have this day so unsparingly rended my soul--had he then addressed me in such accents--it might have been otherwise! Gabriel Süss, Gabriel Süss, the poor, ill-used, rejected, down trodden,--Gabriel Süss, who has torn himself from the blissful faith of his childhood, Gabriel Süss, who has sought and never found forgetfulness of the past amid the roar of cannon and the turmoil of battle.--Gabriel Süss *might have been a support to the wavering, a teacher of his people, a lofty example of humble resignation to the will of God.... His fate was in his own hands. It was his own fault that he perished!...* That was what you said, Michoel; but it was too late!... but no! no! I am not, I am not guilty of it.... that is your invention, ye believers in God!... Naught but a malicious, evil chance swayed me, and even at this critical moment would embitter the sweet instant of revenge by a deceitful image of what I might have been.... just as I am hastily setting forth to accomplish my long-coveted revenge, it lets me meet Michoel Glogau!--Oh! it is naught but malicious evil chance! at the moment, when still irresolute I am for the last time imploring thee, whom men call all-mighty, all-merciful,--in the deepest sorrow, that ever crushed a poor human soul, to restore my father to me, a father! a favour that is not refused to the humblest man on earth-

-at the moment, when I am calling upon thee to restore my father to me, were it but for the shortest interval of time that the human mind is capable of conceiving--to permit me to die in his arms, were it at the penalty of unutterable physical anguish.... *At that moment, I learn that he is dead!...* Where is thy omnipotence? Where? Bow my stiff neck! shatter my pride! conduct me to my father! and I, Gabriel Süss will return unto thee--dost thou hear? to thee, to faith in thee.... I will repent, and dying will glorify thy name!... but it will not be so--the Grave never gives back its dead.... *I was only unexpressibly unfortunate.... and I cry aloud: there is no...."*

Gabriel stopped short. A death-like stillness had reigned round about over the then almost deserted Hahnpass, bounded, as it was, by the spacious graveyard, but suddenly a voice issuing from the burial ground, fell upon his ears, a voice which already once before had made his blood run cold with horror, and which he had then accounted an offspring of his heated over-excited imagination.... but this time it sounded clearer; this time it could be no deception.

"My son! my son! Thou, poor, forsaken one, thou that wert born in sin, where art thou? Where shall I seek thee? Oh! that my voice might echo with the power of thunder, that it might reach from one end of the earth to the other.... perchance my poor son would hear the voice of his father and forgive him!..."

Thus it rung in Gabriel's ears. A hollow cry escaped from his breast, he let fall the latch of the house-door which he had held nervously clutched in his hand.--He looked around, a moderately high wall divided him from the burial ground. Suddenly he perceived a small locked door in the wall, and the intensity of his excitement gave a giant strength to the man naturally powerful: at one blow the boards of the door fell in with a crash, and Gabriel found himself in the cemetery.... His flaming eyes flew over the wide snow-covered space. It was profoundly dark, the sky was obscured by thick clouds, the crumbling grave-stones made a strange contrast with the glittering snow-field; the old trees with their frosted branches like hoary sentinels over this place of rest, floated on the grey atmosphere of the background....

Gabriel put his whole soul in ear and eye:--but for a while saw nothing, heard nothing, not a leaf stirred....

Presently there was a movement among the trees close to him. A feverish heat coursed through his veins: he tottered, but recovered himself with superhuman force and with lips firm closed, and hands pressed nervously against his overflowing bursting heart, approached the thicket.... Tremblingly he parted the branches, nor observed, that his hands were torn and bleeding: he advanced ever forwards, and at last broke through the wood.... Exactly at the same instant the moon passed from behind the black clouds that had hitherto veiled it, and cast its full light over the tree-enclosed spot....

Gabriel perceived three grave-stones, a large and two smaller ones. *The larger had engraved upon it a hunch of grapes the symbol of a Levi....* a lofty form, an old man had sunk down before the gravestones....

Gabriel wished to press forward, to address the form, to look it face to face.... though it should cost him a thousand lives:--but at that instant the old man's trembling voice again resounded....

Gabriel remained rooted to the ground.

"My God! my Lord! all-merciful, all-gracious God!... have I not yet made atonement for the sin of my youth?.... have I not for years done penitence; suffered, as no other man on earth?... Here at the grave of my dead, early lost, father--here at my twin brother's grave, who loved me so dearly, so infinitely deeply, my brother's, who in that fateful night awoke the inexpressibly bitter grief of remorseful despair.... oh would that I had then died, when with strong grasp you threw from off you the disloyal, the wicked shameless brother, would that I had then met my death from your dear fraternal hand!--but no, thou dear one; thou wert not destined to be a Cain, pure and blessed thou wert one day to close thy eyes in peaceful death.... but I, I woke from what seemed the sleep of death, to never ending nameless torment!... At the grave of the never-to-be-forgotten sweet companion of my youth Carpel, whom I would so gladly have once more folded in my arms ... and who peacefully slumbered under this turf, as I returned in despair to Prague, the city of my blissful innocent youth.... at this grave I have for years made my supplication unto thee all-merciful!... Thou, Omniscient, thou that seest into the depths of my soul, thou knowest, what I have suffered!... And still the cloud of thine indignation is not yet passed away.... Thou shalt not commit adultery stands ever written in my bible.... and never yet has my son hastened to my arms!..."

Gabriel scarcely breathed. Each word made its way to his heart like a flaming sword. In his breast raged a storm of emotion, that can neither be represented, nor described, nor conceived. In the inmost core of his being an infinite, all-embracing destroying change was brought to pass.... light suddenly flashed into his soul, and as the dim eyes of the body accustomed to profound obscurity close themselves painfully, if they suddenly gaze into the glowing fire-streams of a mighty volcano; so closed his spiritual eye for one instant before the impression of this trying moment. He was standing by his unhappy father! this form bowed low by sorrow and misery was his poor despairing father.... the mad Jacob!... the most ardent wish of his soul, the deepest longing of his tormented life was stilled, stilled at the moment in which he had given himself over with wild God-denying insolence to the profoundest despair.... *that was no blind chance*.... Gabriel assayed to speak, but his thought found no expression, his lips no sound.

"Father of all men! forgive me at last," Jacob began again in the most heart-rending accents of deepest despair; and his body seemed to collapse under the weight of his sorrow--"forgive me, Father of all!... I have sinned, I have gone astray, but I have suffered endless anguish, and thou, Father! art all-goodness.... Let me die at length, Father of all men.... let me rest by my dear ones.... forgive her also, the mother of my son.... and as a sign that thou hast forgiven me, restore my son to me, *my son*, before I die.... let me die on his heart.... *I can die only on his heart,* I ask for nothing more!... God! grant me my son!... Oh come to me, my son!... my son, where art thou?"

A silence deep as the grave reigned for a moment; then Gabriel cried: "Father, I am here!"

Both, father and son, stared speechlessly at one another for a space.... that was the image, that Gabriel had been vainly endeavouring for some hours to conjure up, his father, the wandering Jew of Aix, that form which had once imprinted its hot lips on his young forehead, they were all one and the same....

The highest pitch of madness was mirrored for a minute in Jacob's face.... but gradually and gradually the immense overpowering force of the joyful surprise seemed to drive away the evil spirit that hovered over his soul. His burning eyes, out of which madness had flashed, became wet.... a hot tear escaped from under his eyelashes and trickled slowly down his pale cheeks....

On a sudden, as if a ray of recognition had then for the first time struck him, he exclaimed, "he bears the fiery sign on his forehead! My God! it is my son!..."

"My father!... Hear oh Israel, the Lord our God is one God."

Gabriel flung himself into his father's wide opened arms.... they held one another in close embrace.... their lips quivered as if they would have spoken.... but they never spoke again.... the too swift alternation of feeling had loosened the slight bond that united spirit to body; the most terrible emotion, that has ever possessed a human heart, killed them!

They held one another still fast embraced in death--in life divided, isolated, *in death they would not be parted.*

This heart-breaking scene had not remained unwitnessed. Blume had stood at the window of her house in sad painful expectation.... What she had seen and heard had filled her with unutterable horror.... but she was saved.... Profoundly struck by this dispensation of Providence, she fell with unspeakable emotion upon her knees and prayed.

Chapter VII

The Palatine escaped next morning in the direction of Breslau. Anhalt, Hohenlohe, the elder Thurn, the elder Bubna, Bohuslaw Berka, Raupowa, and others accompanied him.--The Kleinseiters always devoted to the Emperor, as soon as Frederick had left the city sent messengers to Duke Maximilian and begged him to make his entry into the city. At mid-day the Duke accompanied by Boucquoi and Tilly marched through the Strahower Gate to the Hradschin, William of Lobkowiz, and five other Bohemian nobles came to meet him, wished him joy of the victory that he had won, and begged, as the chronicles declare, in a long speech interspersed with much weeping, pardon for their revolt, the maintenance of their liberties and mercy for the city. Maximilian answered benignantly that he would do all that he was able, and that the city should not be injured; with regard to the other points, he had no full powers. For himself he advised them to surrender unconditionally to the Emperor.--The Alt- and Neu-stadters had sent at the same time a deputation to the Duke, with a request, that he would grant them three days to draw up the conditions, under which they were willing to surrender. Maximilian refused this delay, and they immediately took an oath of obedience and fidelity to the Emperor and delivered up their arms to the duke.--The news of the duke's successful entry had evoked the most joyous excitement in the Jews-town, which like the Kleinseiters had ever been well disposed towards the Emperor. The overseer invited the elders and members of the college of Rabbis to an extraordinary conference at the Rathhaus, and it was unanimously decided, to present a congratulating address to the Duke Maximilian, as victor, in the name of the Jewish community at Prague. The meeting was just at an end, when the grave-diggers accompanied by Cobbler Abraham urgently begged to be admitted. In the morning at a funeral two dead bodies had been found in the burial ground, that held one another close clasped even in death. The two corpses had assumed in death an extraordinary likeness, a likeness such as one only meets with between father and son, both namely bore upon their forehead a similar blue streak. The mad Jacob had been known to everyone, but with regard to the other body only one of the persons who happened to be present at the funeral, could give accurate information. Cobbler Abraham to wit, declared that he had been acquainted with the young man, who had only lately arrived at Prague, and that immediately on his arrival he had recommended him to a lodging at Reb Schlome Sachs', the upper attendant of the Old-Synagogue. In answer to enquiries made of the last mentioned person later on, he had learnt that the stranger was called Gabriel Mar, and was a clever student from upper Germany. The gravediggers thought it their duty to make a report of this strange occurrence to the college of Rabbis and the overseers of the community, and Cobbler Abraham once again repeated his depositions with respect to the corpse of the young man.

The assembled authorities accounted this matter of sufficient importance to justify their casting a look over the letters which had been found in the clothes of the deceased. The superscription at once excited universal surprise, the letters were addressed to Major-General Otto Bitter and signed Ernest of Mannsfield, General and Field Marshal; their contents referred to the operations of the war and secret plans.... No one knew what to think about it. Some were inclined to believe that Gabriel Mar was a messenger of Mannsfield's, others doubted, for if so, Mannsfield would not have signed his name in full, and held Gabriel to be a spy of the Imperialists, who had somehow or other got possession of these letters; others again believed simply that Gabriel Mar, and Major-General Otto Bitter were one and the same person. They had just got into a lively discussion on this point, when the door of the council-room was suddenly opened and Reb Schlome Sachs and Reb Michoel Glogau entered unannounced.

"You come at the right time," cried the overseer to him--"perhaps you can give us some information about your lodger, who...."

"We come for that very purpose, Reb Gadel!" interposed Reb Schlome.... "but I am too much overcome with what I have just heard. Do you tell them, Reb Michoel, I pray you, you are more composed than I."

The attention of the whole assembly was now directed to Michoel Glogau.

"Yesterday," he began, as concisely as possible, "I saw and conversed for the first time with Gabriel Mar, whose body was found this morning in the graveyard. By a chance concurrence of circumstances I was led to suspect that Gabriel Mar might be one and the same person as Gabriel Süss, who disappeared some years ago. This suspicion became certainty, when I shortly afterwards, hidden behind an angle of the wall, called out his name, and he as if from force of an old habit turned his head and looked about as if he sought the caller; and then as though fearing to betray himself, hurried off. His disguise, his presence in the Jews' quarter might have one of two objects, either to inflict some injury on his former brethren, or to rejoin them and repentantly be reconverted to the faith of his childhood. I resolved to speak with Gabriel Mar before my speedy departure. My words, I know not why, had made a deep impression upon him, I determined to attempt to learn his designs; if they were evil, to thwart them, if good as far as my weak strength permitted, to support them....

"I enquired where he lodged, and some hours afterwards found myself at Reb Schlome Sachs'. He received my communications at first very incredulously; but gradually remembered many peculiarities which had at first struck him in the behaviour of his guest.... His wife some days after his arrival had found him, sunk in deep reflection over a map; she had on the same day seen an officer who strikingly resembled Gabriel, riding out with the young Count Thurn! He himself had heard him talking so strangely in his sleep, that he did not at the time know what to make of it; his whole behaviour had been puzzling.... Reb Schlome Sachs was extraordinarily put out, and asked me what I proposed to do.... I requested him to accompany me to Gabriel's room; I would speak with him at once. Without knowing why, it seemed to me as if every minute that was lost was irrecoverably lost.... We went to his room, it was open, but Gabriel was not in the house. By the light of a lamp that was slowly going out, which he had left standing on the table, we saw a bureau that had been violently broken open, and in it arms; on the ground some old papers were scattered about. Reb Schlome shook violently as he took them up; ... they contained the memorial of his father-in-law, the history of his life.... We noticed the marks of recent tears on some passages.... the manuscripts had lain for years locked up in the bureau, there could not be the slightest doubt, that by some curious coincidence Gabriel had got possession of them. Gabriel, none other, could have read these manuscripts, their contents must have moved him to tears, have made a violent impression on him, at one point indeed he must have flung the papers far away from him: so it seemed to both of us, and the contents of the manuscript proved that we were not mistaken. The manuscript, which we both, Reb Schlome Sachs and I, read throught with the most high wrought attention, revealed astonishing events to us.... Mad Jacob was the father of Gabriel Süss, was a brother of Rabbi Mosche's, a son of the great Rabbi Jizchok Meduro, an uncle of Rabbi Schlome's wife.... A wonderful Providence had conducted Gabriel Süss to the house, where he was to learn his father's history.... a wonderful impenetrable providence brought about his death in the same night in his father's arms, at his grandfather's grave!..."

Michoel was compelled to stop from deep emotion, and handed over Rabbi Mosche's Biography to the assembly.

"This is the Lord's doing and it is marvellous in our eyes," said Rabbi Lippmann Heller, who had taken part in the meeting as assessor to the college of Rabbis, at last after a long pause....

"But are you also aware that Gabriel Süss and Major-General Otto Bitter are one and the same person?" he went on to ask....

"Yes," answered Michoel: "while Reb Schlome was unable from deep feeling to tear himself away from the handwriting of his father-in-law; I carefully examined the room. I found several letters from Count Mannsfield to Major-General Otto Bitter, in one of them he wrote that he sent him, Hebrew letters to look over.... among these I found several letters in German, but written in Hebrew characters. These letters were written from Prague by Blume Rottenberg and directed to her husband.... If I rightly remember, and Gabriel Süss' history was correctly related to me, his intended bride was called Blume Rottenberg, and she married her cousin, her father's brother's son.... Blume Rottenberg must be residing in Prague: so please you, my wise men and reverend teachers, she might be summoned, perhaps she will be able to solve the mysterious obscurity that hovers over the life, and still more remarkably over the death of Gabriel Süss, perhaps she will be able to supply information as to the object of his presence in Prague, and of his disguise."

Michoel's proposition was received with general applause--Blume Rottenberg had lived a retired life in Prague and under an assumed name. Only one person, the owner of the dilapidated house which she inhabited, knew her real name and was able to give information as to where she resided. He happened to be present. Blume Rottenberg was requested to betake herself to the house of the Assessor Reb Lippmann Heller, who was to receive her depositions in the presence of the chief overseer.

Both of them returned two hours afterwards much agitated to the meeting. The whole life of Gabriel Süss, all his past was now laid clear before their eyes.... and Gabriel Süss had died repentant in his father's arms!

It was unanimously decided, to bury them both, father and son, close together by the graves of their family.

It was formerly a custom in Israel, to bury the dead as soon as possible. Jacob and his son were to be immediately laid in the grave. All present, deeply moved by the manifest Providence which had brought about everything so wonderfully, determined to attend the funeral obsequies, and were about to repair to the burial ground. They were just issuing from the Rathhaus, when two horsemen on foam-covered steeds galloped up and halted before it. It was a Captain in the Imperial army accompanied by a younger officer.

"Can I speak with the overseer of your community?" asked the Captain. "Do not be alarmed," he went on to say in a friendly voice, seeing that they had become pale with terror, "no harm will happen to the Jewish community; we know that you are well affected to the Emperor and cleave to your Imperial master with firm unchangeable fidelity, ... but unknown to yourselves, an apostate from your faith, an outlaw, an enemy of the Emperor and Empire, the Mannsfieldian General Otto Bitter has been living for the last few days among you in the Jews-town. He did not escape with the Palatine.--We have every reason for believing that he is here in your town. He is Mannsfield's right hand-man and acquainted with all his plans.... I beseech you, make every effort to deliver him alive into our hands."

"That is impossible," answered the chief overseer after a short pause. "He whom ye seek, by God's wonderful dispensation died this day about midnight full of repentance in the arms of his recovered father. We were just about to lay him in the grave: if it pleases you, Sir Captain! will you not go with us to the burial ground.... to convince yourself that Otto Bitter will never again fight against his Imperial master.... you know him by sight?"

"Of course I do? was I not standing by yesterday, when the most accomplished knight of our army. Count Pappenheim, fell badly wounded by his sword...."

On the short way to the burial ground the chief overseer recounted the history of Gabriel's storm tossed life to the Captain, and the strange events that had suddenly rent the mysterious veil that enveloped it....

The two corpses still locked in a fast embrace lay upon the same bier. It was a most striking sight. The two officers uncovered their heads.--The Captain cast a scrutinizing look over Gabriel's body. "There is no doubt, it is he," he said; then drew a paper out of his breast pocket, which he carefully read over and once more from time to time examined the body with the greatest attention....

"I have said so," he repeated, "there is no doubt, the dead man is Otto Bitter...."

"What are your orders with respect to the corpse?" asked the younger officer, "shall it be transported to the castle that the duke...."

"We fight with the living alone, the dead no more belongs to this world," answered the Captain earnestly. "Otto Bitter was a rebel, an enemy of the Emperor and Empire.... but he was a gallant hero.... May God pardon his sins.... overseer! Give me the letters found upon him, and lay your dead in the grave!"

At twilight on the same day two women, like kind angels, prayed kneeling at Gabriel's grave. Both of them were equally nearly related to the departed. The one was Blume Rottenberg, the woman that he had once madly loved, his mother's sister's daughter, the other Schöndel Sachs, his uncle's daughter.

Blume Rottenberg had suffered fearfully for eight days. She was firmly resolved to sacrifice her life rather than her duty.... She had been saved by a miracle. Her trust in God had been thereby still more exalted. She had remained four months without tidings of her husband, and yet looked forward full of trust and hope to the future.... she had not deceived herself. On the 26th of March 1621 the Mannsfieldian commanders surrendered the city of Pilsen to General Tilly and eight days afterwards Aaron Rottenberg returned to the arms of his wife happy, and uninjured.... on his arrival he was surprised by joyful news. Important intelligence for him had come in from Worms. The patrician, who had had that law-suit so full of evil consequences with the Rottenberg family, was dead. Sorely tormented by the stings of conscience he had declared upon his death bed in the presence of his confessor and an officer of justice, that the claim of the Rottenbergs against him was perfectly well grounded, and that the acknowledgment, that he had declared to be forged, was genuine. He further confessed that the heads of the trades had intended to force the Rottenbergs at all hazards to admit that the acknowledgment was forged. This admission was to have been the signal for a general bloody persecution and plundering of the Jews. The reckless project had miscarried owing to the noble firmness of the Rottenbergs. The occasion was seized for an act of private revenge, if illegal at any rate apparently of common advantage, and if the insurgents had succeeded in stirring up the wild fury of a populace eager for plunder, the innocent Jews could at least reckon upon the assistance of the Prince and the sympathy of every right thinking person.... after the dying man had once more solemnly declared, that all his possessions were in justice the property of Aaron Rottenberg, he implored those who were present, with hot tears and in the most moving terms to hunt out the traces of Aaron Rottenberg, not only to put him in possession of his property, but also to tell him that they had been witnesses of the deep contrition and earnest repentance which had embittered his last hours: thus he hoped to obtain pardon from the Rottenbergs, whom his covetousness had plunged in unutterable misery....

Those who had been present at the patrician's death-bed immediately imparted his confession to the authorities of the Jewish community in Worms. This event caused immense excitement there, now for the first time they saw how falsely, how unjustly they had interpreted the noble behaviour of the Rottenbergs, for what heavy injustice they had to ask forgiveness of them. In a meeting of the elders it was unanimously decided to search out Aaron Rottenberg, to ask in the name of the community his forgiveness of the injuries it had inflicted upon him, and urgently to beg him to return to his paternal city, and again to accept the office of an overseer, which his father formerly, and afterwards he himself had filled.

The letter of the Worms community that put him in possession of all these facts, made a most pleasing impression upon Rottenberg. The profound regret, the sorrowful repentance which the community expressed in earnest words, made it impossible for him to oppose their request. He set out on the journey to Worms with a heart full of thankfulness. He was received in his native city with loud rejoicing and trod its streets with tears of emotion....

A long series of happy years effaced from the memory of the Rottenberg family the sorrows of their past life, but not the miracle which the Lord had vouchsafed to them.

Cobbler Abraham looked upon himself with no small pride as an instrument of divine Providence. It was he who had first accosted Gabriel Süss on his arrival in the Jews-town. It was he who had shown him the way to Reb Schlome Sachs, where Gabriel had at last found the solution of the mystery of his life; a solution that had affected him so profoundly, had agitated the inmost depths of his being.--Even fifty years later, when old as Methusalem but still vigorous, Cobbler Abraham was always ready to recount the history of Gabriel Süss to whoever wished it, and only regretted that he could no longer introduce his two former neighbours, Hirsch, the fish-monger, and Mindel, the liver-vender, who had predeceased him, as witnesses to the accuracy and truthfulness with which he described his first meeting with Süss.

Reb Schlome Sachs and his wife lived as before peaceful and contented, and when Schöndel after ten years of childless wedlock was brought to bed of a boy, and so the profoundest, if silent, wish of her heart was fulfilled; nothing was wanting to her perfect happiness....

Michoel Glogau went to Breslau, and taught the word of God there.